"And I'm definit
In fact, I'm hop

D0468958

Tanner pulled his hands from ~~his p~~
another step backward. She was killing him with
her come-hither gaze and words of encouragement
to continue the madness.

"It won't happen again, Josie. I think we both have
enough serious issues going on in our lives. We
don't need to mix in a relationship that will go
nowhere and would only complicate things," he
said firmly.

He hated how quickly her smile disappeared and
the gold sparkle in her eyes faded, but somebody
had to inject cold, hard reality into the crazy
conversation.

And the cold, hard reality was that, despite his
desire for her, he had no place in his life for a young
woman like Josie. She would be a mistake and he
wasn't willing to make that error again. There was
no place for any woman in his life.

* * *

We hope you enjoy this dramatic miniseries:
The Coltons of Texas: Finding love and buried
family secrets in the Lone Star State...

* * *

If you're on Twitter, tell us what you
think of Harlequin Romantic Suspense!
#harlequinromsuspense

Dear Reader,

I love the Coltons series, and *Colton Cowboy Hideout* introduces a new branch of the family. You know there's going to be plenty of drama and danger when the Coltons are in the house!

After the patriarch of the family, a billionaire baron, goes missing the finger-pointing begins among his children and stepchildren. Everyone appears to have a motive...except Josie Colton and Tanner Grange.

Josie has come to the Colton Valley Ranch on a mission and circumstances instantly throw her together with ranch foreman Tanner. The attractive Josie is the last thing Tanner, single father to twin girls, needs in his life. But, when danger appears, Tanner swears to keep her safe and then tell her goodbye.

As far as I'm concerned, there's nothing sexier than a hot cowboy who loves his children and protects his woman...unless it's the hot Italian man I married.

Happy reading!

Carla Cassidy

COLTON COWBOY HIDEOUT

Carla Cassidy

HARLEQUIN® ROMANTIC SUSPENSE

Special thanks and acknowledgment are given to Carla Cassidy for her contribution to the Coltons of Texas miniseries.

ISBN-13: 978-0-373-27994-4

Recycling programs for this product may not exist in your area.

Colton Cowboy Hideout

Printed in U.S.A.

www.Harlequin.com

Carla Cassidy is an award-winning, *New York Times* bestselling author who has written more than one hundred and twenty novels for Harlequin. In 1995, she won Best Silhouette Romance from *RT Book Reviews* for *Anything for Danny*. In 1998, she also won a Career Achievement Award for Best Innovative Series from *RT Book Reviews*. Carla believes the only thing better than curling up with a good book to read is sitting down at the computer with a good story to write.

Books by Carla Cassidy

Harlequin Romantic Suspense

Cowboys of Holiday Ranch

A Real Cowboy
Cowboy of Interest
The Colton Bodyguard
Cowboy Under Fire
Cowboy at Arms

Men of Wolf Creek

Cold Case, Hot Accomplice
Lethal Lawman
Lone Wolf Standing

Cowboy Café

Her Cowboy Distraction
The Cowboy's Claim
Cowboy with a Cause
Confessing to the Cowboy

Chapter 1

She was definitely out of her element. Josie Colton had known that the Colton Valley Ranch just outside of Dallas in Brush Valley was a multibillion-dollar operation, but she hadn't really processed just how well-off this branch of the family was until now.

The early July sun gleamed on the large black ornate gates with COLTON VALLEY RANCH in gold lettering just in front of her car. Beyond the gates in the distance a white, two-story mansion with one-story wings on either side sprawled across a manicured lawn with a regal grace that screamed of wealth and privilege.

For just a brief moment Josie wanted to back up, turn around and leave. She wasn't prepared to meet these people who were family, but strangers nevertheless. After seven years in the witness protection plan, she scarcely felt ready to face her own new life of freedom.

She gripped the steering wheel tightly and remembered that all of her siblings were counting on her. She wasn't here for a social visit; she was here to do a job and she definitely didn't want to disappoint the family she had been reunited with so recently.

She pulled closer to the gates and noticed a speaker built into the column to her left. She rolled down her window and leaned partway out, the sun already hot despite the fact that it was only eight in the morning. Since it was Monday she hoped she'd arrived early enough that Eldridge Colton hadn't already left the house for business purposes.

"Hello?" she called.

"May I help you?" a disembodied male voice replied.

"Hmm, I'm Josie Colton and I believe I'm expected."

The gates opened as if by magic and Josie pulled through. She glanced in her rearview mirror to see them closing behind her.

At least there didn't appear to be anyone following her. For the past couple of weeks more than once a creepy-crawly feeling had suffused her, making her look over her shoulder for some phantom bogeyman.

"No bogeyman," she said firmly and shoved the thought out of her head.

When she'd spoken to her distant cousin, Eldridge Colton, the night before, she had told him exactly what she wanted and why she needed his permission to be on his land. He hadn't hidden a touch of amusement at her request, but had agreed to allow her access to the property.

Now here she was, and despite all she'd been through in her twenty-three years of life, nerves jumped and bubbled in the pit of her stomach.

She parked in the driveway and got out of her car. A light, hot breeze sent her long dark hair flying into unruly disarray and before she rang the doorbell she reached up to smooth the strands.

She was still finger-combing her hair and gathering her nerve when the door opened to reveal a tall, thin older man. Clad in a dark suit, crisp white shirt and gray tie, he sported a gray mustache and a bald head covered with a few thin wisps of gray hair.

"Eldridge?" she ventured tentatively.

"No, ma'am, I'm Aaron Mansfield, the butler." He opened the door wider to allow her entry. "If you'll wait here, I'll see if Mr. Eldridge is available to see you."

He turned and disappeared down a hallway as Josie gazed around at her surroundings. The huge foyer not only sported gorgeous marble floors, but there were also twin curved staircases that swept down from the second floor and nearly stole her breath away with their grand beauty.

She had been raised in a foster home and was

most recently suspected of being a serial killer like her father. After spending seven years in the witness protection program in the small town of Excelsior Springs, Missouri, it would have been easy for her to be overwhelmed and intimidated by the opulence that surrounded her.

But Josie was a survivor and she was on a mission. She'd already been through more difficult times in her life than most people suffered in an entire lifetime. She refused to be cowed by anything or anyone. For the first time ever her family was depending on her to do a job and she didn't want to blow it. She straightened her shoulders and raised her chin as Aaron Mansfield approached her once again.

"Mr. Eldridge is still sleeping, but his wife, Mrs. Whitney, has agreed to see you in the parlor. Please follow me."

He led her to a set of ornate double doors off the foyer. He opened them and gestured for her to enter. Josie swallowed a small gasp of surprise as she got her first sight of Eldridge's wife.

Whitney Colton was clad in an emerald green dressing gown and lounged on a white chaise. Her shoulder-length blond hair was perfectly coiffed and her makeup was impeccable, enhancing her delicate features and bright green eyes. Josie knew Eldridge was seventy-five years old. His wife was at least two decades younger than him.

"Don't dawdle. Come in," Whitney said and waved a hand airily toward a nearby chair.

Josie quickly walked across the room to the chair and sank down. "Hello, I'm Josie Colton and I'm here to—"

"I know why you're here," Whitney interrupted. "My Dridgey-pooh told me all about you last night after you called him."

Dridgey-pooh? Josie inwardly groaned.

"It's so nice to meet a part of the family we don't know," Whitney said with a warm smile.

Josie relaxed against the back of the chair. "Thank you. It's nice to meet you, too. I really appreciate you all allowing me access to your property."

"Dridgey-pooh said it was okay, so I suppose it's okay. He told me all about your family. He said your father spent some time here when he was younger."

"Yes, although it was about twenty years ago or so," Josie replied.

Whitney leaned forward, her eyes gleaming with a sudden hardness. "Tell me, Josie, how does it feel to be the daughter of an infamous serial killer? Oh, I probably shouldn't have asked that. It was rude, wasn't it? Please don't be upset with me."

The question might have been rude, but it was obvious the woman wanted an answer. And how on earth did one answer a question like that?

"It's been rather difficult," Josie finally replied.

Whitney's mouth pursed in a slight pout. She was obviously not pleased with the shortness of Josie's response. Her eyes suddenly widened and she leaned back against the chaise, her perfectly arched eye-brows raised in an unmistakable expression of fear.

"I certainly hope you don't share any crazy hom-icidal tendencies with your father." Her voice was suddenly breathy.

"You don't have to worry—" Josie didn't get the entire sentence out of her mouth before Whitney in-terrupted again.

"I don't really like the idea of you being here at all, but the very last thing I want is to make you mad at me."

Josie's brain ping-ponged in her head with Whit-ney's mercurial mood swings. Did the woman have some kind of mental problem? What was her deal? Before she could respond Aaron appeared in the doorway once again.

"Tanner is here to see you." He no sooner got the words out of his mouth when a tall, blond man in worn tight jeans and a white T-shirt swept past the butler and into the room.

An unexpected butterfly took flight in the pit of Josie's stomach as he gazed at her with the blue eyes of a cloudless Texas sky.

He gave a curt nod in greeting and then turned to Whitney. "I'm sorry to interrupt but I just wanted to let you know that Clementine birthed her foal early this morning and both are doing well."

"Thank you, Tanner, and I am so glad you're here." She pointed to Josie. "This is Jodie Colton, one of Eldridge's very distant cousins. She's here to find a watch or something that is buried on the property. You can see to it that she gets what she needs as quickly as possible."

There was still a touch of breathless distress in Whitney's voice and it was obvious by her words that she wanted Josie gone sooner rather than later. So much for the warmth of her initial greeting, Josie thought.

The man walked over to Josie and held out a hand. "I'm Tanner Grange, the ranch foreman."

Josie rose and shook his hand, the butterfly turning dizzying somersaults at the brief physical contact with his warm, slightly calloused hand. "Hi, I'm Josie Colton and it's nice to meet you."

"Jodie… Josie." Whitney released a musical burst of laughter. "All I know is that it's a beautiful Monday morning and Eldridge and I have a breakfast to attend downtown, but before I get ready I need my guava-kale smoothie. Tanner, see that Josie gets whatever she needs and let me know when she's off the property." She turned on the lounge to face the doorway. "Bettina, bring me my smoothie."

Her last sentence was screamed and Josie didn't miss the slight roll of Tanner's gorgeous eyes. "Shall we?" He gestured toward the door to leave.

With pleasure. Josie didn't mind getting down to business and putting the dramatic, temperamental Whitney behind her. As Josie followed the hunk out of the parlor, she couldn't help but notice his slightly faded jeans looked awesome on his taut butt, as did his T-shirt, which was pulled tight across his broad shoulders.

Get a grip. The very last thing she wanted or needed in her life at the moment was any kind of a romantic connection. Besides, Tanner Grange looked old enough and was definitely hot enough to already be married.

He led her back into the foyer, where he stopped and turned to face her. His handsome, chiseled features formed a slight frown across his forehead that did nothing to detract from his attractiveness. "I'm afraid I have no clue exactly what I'm supposed to help you with. Whitney didn't explain it very well."

"She was worried about her guava-kale smoothie," Josie said drily and then bit her tongue. She had no idea what this man thought about his boss and the last thing Josie wanted to do was make a bad impression or alienate the man who had been tasked to help her.

She was relieved when Tanner offered her a wry grin. "Whitney does love her smoothies, among other fairly superficial creature comforts." His smile fell into a gaze of curiosity. "So, she mentioned something about a buried watch?"

Josie nodded. "My siblings and I were told our father buried a watch here years ago on this property. My father is a second cousin to Eldridge and spent some time here when he was younger. He's dying now and the watch has sentimental value to him and he'd like to be buried with it, so I'm here to hopefully find it."

There were a million things Josie didn't say, like that her father was in prison, convicted of killing nine men and Josie's own mother. She also didn't mention that she and her siblings believed the watch might hold a map that could possibly lead to her father's stash of money from old bank heists he had committed before he went to prison twenty years ago.

"I'm sorry about your father."

"Thanks," Josie replied. "He's been sick for a long time."

"This is a big spread. Do you have any idea where this watch might be?"

"It's supposed to be at the base of an old oak tree with some kind of carvings in the trunk and the tree is near a brook or a stream."

Whitney's strident voice drifted out to them. "Moira, wake up Eldridge. He needs to get ready for the fundraising breakfast downtown."

Tanner frowned. "I think I know that particular tree. It's in a pasture a bit of a distance away from the house. Do you ride?"

"Ride? You mean like on a horse?" Josie shook her head. "I'm afraid I've never had the opportunity."

"That's all right. We can take one of the ranch trucks. Shall we?" He gestured toward the front door.

Josie was just about to step outside when a blood-curdling scream pierced the air.

Adrenaline pumped through Tanner as he recognized the scream as coming from the housekeeper,

Moira. "Excuse me," he muttered to Josie and turned to race down the hallway toward the master suite.

He was vaguely aware of Aaron, Whitney and the pretty petite Josie following right behind him. Dread coursed through him as he saw Moira standing just outside of the doorway of the bedroom.

She held a trembling finger to her lips and looked every day of her seventy-five years. As she saw Tanner she pointed into the room, horror gripping her features into a tight mask.

At his age, Eldridge wasn't in the best of health and Tanner's first thought was that the old man had probably passed away in his sleep.

He flew into the large room and then froze in his tracks in stunned surprise. In an instant his brain registered several things. The window to the gardens was open and the screen had been removed. The lamp on the nightstand was overturned. The covers on the bed appeared to have been dragged off and something that looked like blood was both on the windowsill and on the floor next to the bed.

Eldridge was gone.

"Oh, my God!" Whitney screamed from behind Tanner. "Where is he? What's happened?" She pushed past Tanner and ran into the adjoining bathroom. "Eldridge honey, where are you?" A wail ensued, letting Tanner know the old man wasn't there.

Whitney stumbled back into the bedroom, and at the same time Fowler Colton, Eldridge's eldest son, ran into the room. He was followed by his sister, Alanna.

Bedlam ensued as more of the Colton family appeared on the scene. Zane, Eldridge's adopted son and head of security, shouted to be heard above Whitney's hysterical screams.

Within minutes all of Whitney and Eldridge's children and stepchildren were in the room except one. Aaron held on to his wife, Moira, his eyes misted with tears, and Josie cowered against a wall as if attempting to disappear.

"Everyone out of the room," Reid Colton yelled above the din. "We need to preserve the evidence." He attempted to herd everyone back out into the hallway.

"I just called Sheriff Watkins," Fowler replied. "He's on his way. In the meantime, I need to take a look around."

"No, you don't. You need to get out of here like everyone else," Reid replied tersely.

"Don't act like you're a cop. You just used to be one," Fowler replied with a raise of his chin. "As I remember, brother, your badge was taken away from you."

Reid stared menacingly at Fowler and one of his hands tightened into a fist. "Don't go there, brother."

"You two, don't even start," Whitney cried. She started out of the door and then stopped and stared at Josie. "You! You did this. You brought evil into the house. It's all your fault. You're the devil!" She covered her eyes and wept as her daughter Piper placed an arm around her shoulders and quickly led her from the room.

Josie's hazel eyes were wide and her lower lip began to tremble. Tanner fought the crazy impulse to shelter her with his arm. Instead he motioned for her to follow him out of the bedroom and fought against his worry for the old man he'd looked on like a father.

"Everyone into the parlor," Fowler instructed. "Sheriff Watkins will want to question everyone when he and his men get here."

"I don't think it's a good idea for Josie to be in the parlor with Whitney," Tanner said. "I'll take her into the dining room and we'll wait there for the sheriff."

Josie gave him a grateful glance. He didn't wait for permission from anyone, but took her by the arm and led her in the opposite direction from the rest of the people. The last thing needed at the moment was Whitney's histrionics directed toward Josie.

As they walked toward the formal dining room Tanner tried to tamp down his fear for Eldridge. What on earth had happened in that bedroom?

It had been obvious that a struggle had occurred. Had it happened that morning? Sometime in the night? Had the old man been kidnapped? Had he been killed? There hadn't been a lot of blood to indicate a death, but there had certainly been enough for Tanner to be extremely concerned about Eldridge's well-being.

The formal dining room was a large room with a

table that nearly stretched from one end to the other. Several large candelabras were positioned on a black-and-gold table runner and held fat, white pillar candles.

This was where the large family usually gathered to take their evening meal together. Breakfast and lunch were less formal. He gestured Josie into one of the high-backed chairs and then sank down in the chair next to her.

Josie's scent wafted toward him, a heady combination of spices mingling with a fresh peach fragrance. He'd experienced a swift kick of physical attraction to her the moment he'd first laid eyes on her. Her long dark hair looked silky, and she might be small and petite, but her body was perfectly proportioned. But at the moment that was the last thing on his mind.

He reached up and rubbed the center of his forehead, where a headache attempted to take hold. Loud voices could still be heard coming from the parlor, where the family and other staff members were gathered together.

"Whatever happened in that bedroom, I'm in no way responsible," Josie said. Her eyes simmered as she held his gaze. He couldn't help but notice her eyelashes were lush and long.

"I'm aware of that. I just wish I knew what really did happen."

"There were so many people. Are all of them family?"

He nodded. "Eldridge had two children, Fowler and Alanna, with his first wife, Darla. When Darla died Eldridge married Whitney, who had two children, Zane and Marceline. Eldridge and Whitney had three children together, Thomas, Piper and Reid. Well, actually, Piper was an orphan who they adopted. The only one who wasn't in the bedroom a few minutes ago was Marceline."

"Thank goodness I won't be here long enough to try to keep them all straight," Josie replied.

"They all have very distinct personalities, so once you've been around them for a short period of time it's fairly easy to figure out who is who," he replied. It was easier to focus on the Colton family dynamics rather than his fear for his boss and mentor.

The faint shriek of sirens was audible from somewhere outside, and before they halted their cry, Brianna Nugent flew into the dining room.

Tanner jumped out of his chair at the sight of his young nanny. "Brianna, what are you doing in here? Where are the girls?" A new concern whipped through him. Had something happened to them?

"Peggy said she'd watch them for a few minutes," Brianna replied and tugged on the end of the thick blond braid that fell forward over her shoulder. "What's going on? There's so much negative energy in the air. It's totally upsetting my chakra."

Tanner drew in a breath and sought some modicum of patience before replying. "Eldridge is missing. I'm sorry about your chakra, but you really need to get back to the girls."

"Do you mind if I burn some sage in the nursery to clear away some of the bad energy?"

Tanner stared at her in disbelief. "You are not to burn anything in the nursery ever," he replied firmly. "Now, I'd appreciate it if you'd get back to the twins. The negative air in here is far worse than any in the staff wing." As Brianna whirled back out of the room, Tanner sat once again and released a deep sigh.

"You have twin daughters?" Josie asked.

Tanner relaxed a bit. It was impossible to feel too stressed out when he thought about his little girls. "Lily and Leigh—they're eighteen months old. Brianna is their nanny."

"So your wife works outside of the home?"

"My ex-wife, and she died a little over a year ago." He fought against the sense of failure that always tried to take hold of him when he thought of Helen.

"Oh, I'm so sorry," Josie replied.

"Thanks." He leaned forward, tension once again twisting inside of him. "I just hope Brianna doesn't let her unsettled chakra affect the twins. Kids pick up on grown-ups' emotions so easily, and the last thing I want is for them to be upset."

He also knew with a sinking sensation that Brianna, with her slightly crazy new age mentality, was probably going to have to be replaced. Anyone who thought burning sage in the nursery was okay wasn't the kind of nanny he wanted for his girls.

He shoved the thought aside and looked at Josie once again. "What about you? Are you married? Have children?" Although Josie looked far too young for either, he wanted—needed—some conversation to keep his mind busy until the sheriff or somebody else official came in to speak with them.

"Neither," she replied.

"Do you have other family?"

"Five brothers and a sister, but my mother died when I was three and we had an absent father, so we were all separated and grew up in different foster-care homes."

"Foster care can be tough. It must have been especially difficult being separated from your brothers and sister."

She stared down at the tabletop and traced an imaginary pattern on the wood with her fingertip. "It was, but you know what they say—when you're handed lemons make lemonade."

She dropped her hand into her lap and looked up at him again. "By the time I was six there were five other foster kids living in the same house as me. I made them my brothers and sisters and tried to take good care of them. What about you? Do you have other family?"

"It's just me and my daughters," he replied.

Eldridge was missing under mysterious circumstances. Josie Colton stirred something inside Tanner that hadn't been stirred in a long time. Then there was the worry that he probably needed to hire a new nanny…again.

He was almost relieved when Sheriff Troy Watkins appeared in the doorway. "Tanner, I need to ask you both some questions." The tall, dark-haired lawman pulled a notepad and pen out of his shirt pocket and then looked at Josie, his gray eyes flat and emotionless.

"Josie Colton, I understand you arrived at the ranch just before Eldr—Mr. Colton was found missing. Where were you last night?"

"I was at my apartment in Granite Gulch. I got up early this morning to drive in," Josie replied. "If they have security cameras around the area, then I'm sure they'll show you precisely when I arrived here."

"And you're one of Mr. Colton's cousins?" Troy asked.

"We're third cousins. I've never even met him. I just spoke to him on the phone last night. He agreed to let me come here and search for an old watch that belongs to my father."

Troy turned to look at Tanner. "And what about you, Tanner? Where were you in the hours before Eldridge was found missing?"

"I spent the night in the barn. We had a horse that foaled and I didn't leave the barn until this morning when I came into the house to speak with Whitney. She introduced me to Josie and here we are. Several of the ranch hands were in and out of the barn all night," Tanner explained. "They can tell you I was in the barn until this morning."

"I only planned on being here today," Josie said.

"Your plans have now changed," Troy replied flatly. "I don't want you leaving here until we've conducted a more thorough investigation."

He turned back to look at Tanner. "Whitney told me to tell you to find accommodations for Ms. Colton in the staff wing and to see that she has whatever she needs."

Tanner stifled a sigh. As if he didn't already have enough chaos in his brain, he'd now been given a babysitting duty for a very hot young woman whose lower lip trembled slightly. Her eyes had darkened with what suspiciously looked like secrets.

Chapter 2

It was like watching a mystery movie where Josie didn't know the actors and definitely couldn't get a grasp on the plot. Eldridge was missing, Whitney thought she was the devil incarnate and the only oddly comforting element in the craziness was the tall, rather stoic man beside her whom she'd met only an hour or so ago.

Evil. You came from evil and that blood runs through your veins. She mentally shook her head to dispel the inner voice that haunted her more often than she wanted to admit.

She'd been grateful that the sheriff hadn't asked any questions about her father. Her first impulse now was to jump in her car and get out of here as fast as possible, but with the sheriff's admonition not to leave the property ringing in her ears, that wasn't an option.

Even though she'd never met Eldridge she was concerned for his safety, but she couldn't believe she was now under some sort of house arrest until further notice.

"Come on. I'll show you to the staff quarters," Tanner said. "Besides, I'm eager to check in on my daughters."

She followed him out of the dining room and into a labyrinth of hallways that led farther away from the family's living space.

"The left wing is where Fowler and Alanna live," he explained as they walked. "In the main house Eldridge and Whitney have the first-floor suite and everyone else has suites on the second floor. This right wing is for some of the staff."

"None of the children are married?" she asked.

"As far as I know, none of them are even close except maybe Fowler. He's had a girlfriend forever, but so far they aren't even engaged yet."

"Fowler's the oldest, right?"

Tanner nodded. "He's the president of Colton Incorporated and a genius at business wheeling and dealing."

Josie frowned. From what small interaction she'd seen between all of them, Fowler had appeared to be a bit of a pompous jerk.

"Feel free to check on your daughters before you

show me to a room," Josie said as they turned down another long hallway.

He flashed her a grateful smile over his muscled shoulder. "Thanks. I appreciate it."

No, thank you. Oh, she could definitely get used to his beautiful smiles. But, of course, she hoped she wouldn't be here long enough to get used to anything. Hopefully she'd find the watch and then the sheriff would allow her to go home before the end of the day.

They continued down several more hallways before he stopped in front of a door. "This is my suite," he said and then opened the door to allow her into a small but inviting living room with a kitchenette area.

The room was decorated in warm earth tones and the brown sofa held not only a couple of yellow throw pillows, but also a plastic baby doll and a little bedraggled stuffed dog. Two high chairs sat side by side on the small square of tiled area just in front of a window next to the refrigerator.

The sound of crying babies drifted out from another room. Josie followed him through the living room, past what was obviously the master bedroom, and another closed door and then into a smaller room where Brianna stood with one twin in her arms and the other one clinging to her legs. The young nanny looked frantic.

Despite their tears, the twins were beautiful, each with blond curls and big blue eyes. One was clad in pink shorts and a pink-flowered top and the other was dressed all in purple.

The room was obviously not only a place for the twins to sleep, but also where they played. A large wooden box rested between the two cribs and was filled with toys, and a miniature table and chairs in bright primary colors was set against one wall.

"What's going on?" Tanner asked. The little girl in Brianna's arms reached out to him and he took her from the nanny.

Josie didn't hesitate. She leaned down and plucked the other twin from Brianna's legs. "Hi, baby," she said with a big smile. "Are you Lily or Leigh?"

The beautiful blond-haired girl stopped crying and eyed Josie soberly, and then her rosebud lips curled up into a responding smile.

"You have Lily," Tanner said. "Lily wears purple and Leigh wears pink to make it easy for people to tell them apart." He patted Leigh's back as she sniffled a final little hiccuping sob. "How long have they been crying?" He looked at Brianna.

"Just for a couple of minutes," she replied and her pointed chin thrust upward defensively. "It's time for them to go down for their morning nap and they always get a bit crabby around now."

As if to support Brianna's claim, Lily yawned and snuggled closer against Josie's chest. Josie's heart squeezed with a sharp surge of unexpected emotion.

There had never been much softness in Josie's life, but her head was now filled with the scent of sweet baby and Lily's little body warmed not just the front of her blouse, but radiated through the cotton material to heat her heart in a way she'd never felt before.

Tanner gazed at Lily and Josie for a long moment. "If you don't mind, I'll just get them settled down in their cribs before we take off."

"I don't mind at all," Josie replied. "Take all the time you need."

Brianna sat on a tiny chair at a miniature table as Tanner carried Leigh to one of the cribs.

Josie followed his lead and took Lily to the other crib and placed her on the mattress on her tummy. She rubbed Lily's back and Lily scrubbed at her eyes with a balled fist.

Within minutes both girls were sound asleep and Tanner gestured for Brianna and Josie to follow him out of the nursery and back into the living room.

"Has there been any word about Eldridge?" Brianna asked. Her hand worried the end of her braid with sparkling blue-painted fingernails.

Tanner frowned. "No, nothing, but hopefully the sheriff will have some answers for everyone soon. I'll check in later this afternoon." With a nod to Brianna, he then gestured for Josie to follow him out of the suite.

"I'm fairly sure the room next door to mine is empty," he said. He raked a hand through his hair and appeared distracted.

"Before you show me a room, why don't we see if I can dig up the watch? Hopefully by that time the mystery of Eldridge's disappearance will be solved and the sheriff will let me leave and go home," Josie replied.

She had a feeling the last thing Tanner Grange needed was to babysit her. It had been obvious he was concerned about Eldridge and the additional worry over a nanny who wanted to burn sage in a children's nursery. He had enough on his plate without her.

"Are you sure?" he asked. "We could get you settled in here before taking off for that tree."

She shook her head. "Maybe I won't have to get settled in here at all."

"All right, then." He looked slightly relieved.

"I just hate that you have to take the time to show me to that tree."

"It's not a problem. In fact, the distraction will be good for me," he assured her.

Minutes later they were outside in the hot July sun and heading for a black king-cab pickup truck parked by one of the many barns on the property.

"This is some spread," Josie said as she hurried her steps to keep up with his long strides. As far as the eye could see were pastures and outbuildings.

"It is," he agreed. "Someday I'd like to have a ranch of my own, although certainly nothing on this scale. It's my dream to have a place of my own to work, a place my girls can really call home." They reached the truck. "Why don't you go ahead and get in and I'll just grab a shovel from the barn."

As he disappeared into the building, Josie climbed into the passenger seat. The truck interior smelled like Tanner, a heady combination of clean male and woodsy-scented cologne.

When he came back out of the barn, a black cowboy hat covered his head and he carried a shovel. Once again she couldn't help but notice his attractiveness. Nothing better than a man in tight jeans and a cowboy hat, she thought.

The last time she'd experienced this kind of strong magnetic tug toward a man had been when she was sixteen years old and had fallen head over heels in love with Michael Evans. Her heart squeezed tight as old memories of her first and only love washed over her.

She and Michael had been achingly young and full of silly dreams—dreams that had been unable to last under the harshness of her reality.

Her thoughts returned to the here and now and the man who had instantly sparked something inside of her. Tanner Grange had a tough road ahead of him as a single parent. How tragic that he'd lost his ex-wife so young, leaving him as the sole parent to those two beautiful girls.

The shovel clanged noisily as he placed it in the pickup bed and then he got in behind the wheel.

"Your daughters are darling," she said as he started the engine and took off.

"Thanks. They're my entire life." He frowned. "And finding a good nanny for them has been almost impossible. Brianna is the fourth one I've hired in the past six months or so."

"What was wrong with the first three?" Josie asked curiously. She was eager to talk about anything but the fact that there were still several official vehicles parked at the house, indicating that the investigation was ongoing.

"The first woman was too impatient. She snapped at the girls constantly. The second lost one of the twins at the petting zoo we have here on the property, and the one before Brianna thought it was perfectly okay to strap the girls into the chairs at their little table with belts whenever they misbehaved." His jaw tensed. "I know the girls can be a handful, but no way will I tolerate that kind of discipline."

Josie was horrified that anyone would think it was okay to tie up a child anywhere. "That's appalling, but Brianna seems nice enough."

His muscles relaxed a bit. "She's kind to the girls, although I think she gets overwhelmed easily and her chakra is constantly getting out of joint, so there's no telling how long she'll hang around." He shot her a quick glance. "You seem like you're good with children."

A small laugh escaped her. "Other than when I was mothering the little ones in foster care, I've never had an opportunity to be around any before today."

"Then I guess that makes you a natural," he replied.

Josie stared out the passenger window and considered his words. Was she a natural with children? She had no idea what she was good at or where she was going. Until a month ago she hadn't believed she had any kind of a future at all.

At the moment her future held only the need to find the watch and take it back to Granite Gulch so she and her siblings could take it to her father in prison.

She only hoped Eldridge Colton didn't wind up murdered. She'd had more than enough of murder and mayhem to last the rest of her life.

She glanced at Tanner once again. His attention was directed out the window, but a pulse had begun working in his jaw again. She fought against a crazy impulse to lean over and stroke away the knot of tension. "You're worried about Eldridge," she ventured.

He flashed another gaze at her from his amazing blue eyes. "I am. He's a character, and he definitely has enough kids of his own, along with Whitney's kids that he adopted, but he's always treated me as a sort of adopted son.

"I lost my parents in a car accident when I was twenty-two and Eldridge hired me on here and helped fill that void. I was honored when he made me foreman four years ago. I wasn't sure I was ready to take on the responsibility, but he assured me that I was the man he wanted for the job. I care about him deeply." His masculine voice cracked.

"I hope he's found safe and sound," she replied, although she already feared the worst for Eldridge.

There was no question that there had been a struggle and there had been blood. Definitely not a good thing.

"There seemed to be a lot of tension between everyone," she said, breaking the silence that had momentarily risen up between them. "For a minute I thought two of the men were going to have a fistfight."

"Fowler and Reid," he replied. "They don't get along very well. I guess family dynamics can be complicated."

Nobody knew that better than Josie. Her family dynamics had been strange for almost all of her life.

She focused her attention out the window once again as the truck rumbled over rough terrain. They'd left the smoother pasture behind and were headed toward a heavily wooded area.

A burst of anxiety filled her. The last thing she wanted or needed was to become embroiled in a kidnapping or a murder. She'd believed that all evil was finally behind her and she'd never have to think about anyone's murder again. She just hoped by the time she dug up the watch, the mystery at the mansion would be solved and she could go back to Granite Gulch and figure out who she really was and what she wanted from life.

Tanner had a hundred worries on his mind, but in the relatively small confines of the pickup cab his main focus was now on the woman seated next to him.

Something about Josie Colton reminded him that he wasn't just a single father of twin daughters, but he was also a healthy man who had felt alone long before his wife, Helen, had walked out on him.

He cast a quick glance at Josie. The sleeveless blue button-up blouse she wore enhanced the rich darkness of her thick hair and showcased a trim waist and the thrust of her breasts. Although she was short, her legs appeared long and shapely beneath the bottom of the jean shorts she wore.

His fingers tingled with the desire to curl into the silky strands of her long hair. He wondered if her hazel eyes would turn more green or blue or gold when in the midst of a passionate encounter.

He tightened his grip on the steering wheel. What was wrong with him? What in the heck was he thinking? He was in his midthirties and she looked barely legal. Besides, she was here to dig up an old watch and then she'd be on her way. Apparently the trauma of the morning had his brain firing nonsense in his head.

He was grateful when they reached the area where the truck could no longer travel over the heavily wooded landscape. "We'll have to go on foot from here," he said. He shut off the engine and unfastened his seat belt while she did the same.

"Is it far?" she asked.

"About a five-minute walk," he replied. At least

out here the air smelled of trees and nature instead of spices and peaches and Josie.

He frowned down at her pink-polished toenails that peeked out of flimsy-looking gold-trimmed white sandals. "Are you going to be able to walk okay in those?"

She flashed him a cheeky grin. "Women can walk in any footwear, including four-inch heels when necessary. Just lead the way."

He grabbed the shovel from the pickup bed and then, with her trailing just behind him, he forged ahead into the thick woods.

Other than the faint trickle of the brook that ran through this area and an occasional rustle of a rabbit or another small animal racing to find cover, a pleasant quietness reigned. It was especially pleasant after the utter chaos in the house.

He was grateful Josie didn't feel the need to fill the relative silence with meaningless chatter. He needed some time to clear his head and calm his racing thoughts.

Sheriff Troy Watkins certainly didn't have to go far to look for suspects in Eldridge's case. All he had to do was look at the family and he'd find plenty of people who had motive to want to do harm to the old man.

Would a ransom call come in? Would a note be received demanding money for the return of Eldridge? Had a business rival gone over the deep end and sought revenge? Hopefully Troy would be able to figure it out quickly and get Eldridge home safe and sound.

He glanced over his shoulder and stopped in his tracks as he realized Josie had fallen slightly behind. "Sorry," she said with a smile. "My legs aren't as long as yours."

"No problem," he replied and tried to ignore how her beautiful smile warmed something in his stomach that hadn't been warmed for a very long time. "It's not too far now." She stepped up beside him and once again he was taunted by her inviting scent.

"This watch must really be important to your father for you to go to all this trouble," he said. Here in the shade provided by the trees overhead, her eyes gleamed gold-green.

"He wants to be buried with it and my siblings thought it was important to try to get it for him."

"Are your siblings all younger than you?" he asked.

"No, I'm the youngest." Her gaze shot ahead, as if eager to get the job done.

And why wouldn't she be in a hurry? He was sure the last thing she wanted to do was spend any more time in his company. She probably thought he was an old fogy. Hell, he was an old fogy who wanted only peace and stability for his daughters.

He had no desire to hang out in a bar or go dancing at the latest hot spot. He'd rather play on the floor with his daughters than do much of anything else.

They moved ahead and the small stream appeared

next to them, babbling musically over the small rocks in its path. Josie threw a glance over her shoulder and then stumbled over an exposed tree root.

He reached out and grabbed her firmly by the upper arm to steady her. Sensory overload instantly threatened to dizzy his head. Beneath the grasp of his hand her skin was warm and soft. A strand of her hair flew across his cheek, a tease of silkiness that caused tightness in his gut.

Once she was stable, he dropped his grip on her and took a step back. "Thanks," she said, her voice slightly husky.

He gave her a curt nod and once again they walked on. "There it is." He pointed ahead to an ancient oak that rose up majestically next to the stream. The trunk was huge and marred by a series of old carvings dug deep within the wood.

Tension wafted from Josie. "It's just like my father described—the tree, the carvings and the creek."

"Did he tell you what the carvings meant?"

She shook her head. "No. I'm not even sure he's the one who made them."

"Then let's see if we can dig up an old watch," he replied.

They hadn't quite reached the front of the tree when a man stepped out from behind it, a gun in his hand.

Josie released a sharp yelp of surprise and Tanner tightened his grip on the shovel. What in the hell was going on? Did this man have something to do with whatever had happened to Eldridge?

"Josie Colton," he said, his thin lips twisting into a sneer. "I knew if I tailed you long enough you'd lead me to the watch. I've been watching you for days."

"Who are you?" Josie asked.

"That's for me to know and you not to find out," he replied. "Now, about that watch…"

"What watch?" she replied. "I—I don't know what you're talking about." Her voice held a tremor that belied her calm demeanor.

Tanner didn't move a muscle although his brain fired off in a dozen different directions. The man had called her by name, so this obviously had nothing to do with Eldridge.

Why would a man with a gun know about a watch wanted for sentimental reasons? What hadn't Josie told him? Was it possible to unarm the man without anyone getting hurt?

"Don't play dumb with me, girly." The man raised a hand to sweep a lank of oily dark hair out of his eyes. "Your daddy spent years in prison bragging about how he was going to be buried with that cheap watch and then nobody would ever find the map to all the money from those old bank heists." He took a step toward them. "Now, tell me where that watch is. I want that map."

Adrenaline pumped through Tanner. He certainly didn't know anything about old bank robberies, but a sick danger snapped in the air.

A look of deadly menace radiated outward from the gunman's dark, beady eyes. The gun was steady in his hands and Tanner's chest constricted.

He tightened his grip on the shovel, calculated the distance between himself and the gunman's arm and then he swung. The end of the shovel connected. The gun fell from the man's grasp, but not before he fired off a shot.

The woods exploded with sound—the boom of the gun, a flutter of bird wings overhead as they flew out of the treetops and Josie's scream of unmistakable pain.

Chapter 3

Pain seared through Josie's upper arm. She grasped it and warm blood seeped through her fingers. At the same time the man picked up his gun from the ground and then turned and ran, quickly disappearing into the thicket.

Tanner dropped the shovel and his hat fell off his head as he raced to her side. Josie's brain fogged with shock and the stinging agony of her injury.

"Here, take this." Tanner quickly pulled his T-shirt over his head, exposing lean muscle and taut abs. He thrust the shirt into her hand. "Press it against your wound. We need to get back to the truck and get you some medical help." His urgent tone cleared some of the fog from Josie's head.

Help. Yes, she needed help, although some of the excruciating sting had already started to abate. Still, she'd been shot. She'd been shot! The thought momentarily weakened her knees.

Tanner bent down and grabbed the shovel and his hat. Then with narrowed eyes he scanned the area. "Let's get out of here," he said urgently.

As they headed back to the truck Tanner remained vigilant, looking both behind them and around the trees surrounding them even though his shovel would be of little use against another flying bullet.

They didn't speak and Josie heard nothing to indicate they were being tracked, but then she hadn't heard anything before the man had leaped out from behind the oak tree.

The back of her throat threatened to close off and tremors filled her as a chill gripped her very soul. Jeez, she'd been shot. The creepy-crawly feeling she'd had for the last couple of weeks of somebody following her hadn't just been her imagination. There *had* been somebody following her…watching her.

Who was the man? Where had he come from? Apparently he'd followed her all the way from Granite Gulch and she hadn't even known it.

She stumbled across the ground, inwardly screaming. Once again her father was responsible for chaos and danger…a danger she'd brought here to Tanner.

What if he'd been shot? What if he'd been killed? His daughters would have probably wound up in foster care, and the foster-care system had been responsible for Josie needing to go into the witness protection program for so many years.

Who was the man? The question played over and over again in her mind. Was he one of her father's old buddies? How had he known she would lead him to the watch? If Tanner hadn't attacked first, would the man have shot them both if she hadn't produced the watch? Oh, God, what a mess.

By the time they reached the truck, her frantic heartbeat had begun to slow. Tanner helped her into the passenger seat and then he got behind the wheel and started the engine with a roar.

"Are you losing a lot of blood? Are you keeping pressure on the wound? Do you feel like you're going to pass out?" The questions fired out of him as the truck bumped across the land at what felt like a breakneck speed.

"No, I'm not going to pass out." She pulled the T-shirt away from her arm. Blood. Bright red blood, but not as much as she'd expected. "I think the bullet just grazed me." She returned pressure on the wound.

"Hopefully Troy is still at the house. We need to report this."

"No!" She straightened up in the seat and shot him a frantic glance. "Please, don't do that." He cast her a quick frown and she continued, "He can't do anything about this. I'll explain everything to you when we get back to the house. Just please don't get the sheriff involved in this."

He made no reply.

The drive back to the house seemed to take forever. Tears pressed hot behind her eyes. The tears weren't for her. She never cried for herself.

The emotion was the result of the close call they'd just had and because Tanner could have been killed because of her. He was just an innocent bystander thrust into the disaster of her life. He had nothing to do with her, her father, the watch or the danger that had come out of nowhere.

When they reached the house Tanner parked next to the barn where they'd originally started from, and they both got out of the vehicle.

"Let's get you into my suite, where I can take a look at your arm and see if you need real medical care," he said.

Thankfully they managed to make it to his suite without encountering anyone else. Once there he unlocked the door and gestured her inside.

Brianna stepped out of the nursery, took one look at the bloody T-shirt Josie held against her upper arm and turned pale. "Oh, my God, what's happened? How did she get hurt? Did you hurt her?"

"No, I didn't hurt her," Tanner replied with exasperation in his voice. "Brianna, take the girls to the dining room for lunch," he added curtly.

Lunch? Was it just now noon? It felt as if an entire lifetime had passed since she'd pulled up to the front gates to meet Eldridge and his family.

Tanner led her through the master bedroom and into an adjoining bathroom, where he motioned her to have a seat on the commode. He disappeared for a moment and then returned wearing a navy blue short-sleeved pullover shirt.

She sank down, her body once again trembling uncontrollably. Tanner gently pulled the T-shirt from her grasp and released a sigh of obvious relief. "It's already stopped bleeding and I don't think there's a bullet in your arm." He tossed the shirt to the floor and then bent down beneath the sink and retrieved a bottle of hydrogen peroxide and some cotton balls.

"This might hurt a bit," he said and then began to clean the wound.

She closed her eyes and winced as he carefully cleaned the area. Instead of focusing on the pain, she concentrated on the outdoorsy, wonderful scent of him and the tenderness of his touch.

"Thank God it's not worse," he said softly, his breath warm on the side of her face. "You were right—it's just a graze."

She opened her eyes to look at him. "You could have been killed and it would have been all my fault."

"I could have gotten you killed with my kung-fu-fighting imitation," he replied drily. He stepped back from her and grabbed a large bandage and some antibiotic cream.

"You saved my life," she replied. Tears once again blurred her vision as she thought of the moment the man had jumped out with his gun pointed at them.

Tanner's sensual lips thinned and he gently rubbed the antibiotic cream on her and then covered the bullet graze with the bandage. Once finished he stepped back from her and held her gaze. "And now you're going to tell me exactly why an armed man would follow you here and want a watch that has only sentimental value to your dying father. Is your father really dying or was that just a lie?"

She would have liked to take offense at his sharp, skeptical tone, but she knew it was more than warranted after what had just happened. "My father really is dying and he told all of us kids that he wanted the watch for sentimental reasons, but we suspect the watch is more than just a simple keepsake."

The musical laughter of a toddler drifted from the nursery, sending a new wave of horror through Josie. She gazed up at him and once again her vision blurred slightly by impending tears. "For the past couple of weeks I've had the feeling that somebody was following me, but I chalked it up to my overactive imagination. I didn't know I was bringing danger here. I can't believe I might have gotten you killed. I could have been responsible for your daughters becoming orphans."

"But that didn't happen. Come on. Let's get out of here and go into the living room, where we can talk more comfortably." He held out a hand and after a moment of hesitation she grabbed it and allowed him to pull her up from the commode.

They returned to the living room, where he gestured for her to sit on the sofa and he sat in a nearby chair. Brianna appeared pushing a two-seat stroller with the twins jabbering happily.

Tanner didn't speak until Brianna and the girls had left the suite for lunch. "Do you need something cold to drink? Or maybe a cup of hot tea?" he asked.

She shook her head. "No, I'm fine." She touched the bandage over the throbbing gunshot graze. "Thank you for cleaning me up."

He nodded and held her gaze intently. "Now, tell me—why shouldn't we report this to the sheriff?"

Her pale features appeared haunted and she grimaced slightly, whether at his question or because of the wound in her shoulder, he didn't know.

"It's kind of a long story," she finally said.

He leaned back in the chair. "We have all afternoon." He was determined to get answers from her no matter how long it took. After what they'd just been through she definitely owed him some answers.

She held his gaze for a long moment and then focused on some undefinable point just over his shoulder. "Have you heard about the Alphabet Killer?"

"I didn't follow the case closely, but I read something about a serial killer who drew a red bull's-eye on victims' foreheads." Why was she bringing up a heinous case like that? If he remembered right, it had been solved in the last month or so and the killer was now behind bars.

She nodded. "The woman who was finally captured as the killer, Regina Willard, murdered women with long dark hair and marked them with the bull's-eye. Her victims' names were Anna, Brittany and Celia and others following the pattern, so she earned the nickname of the Alphabet Killer."

"Okay, but what does that have to do with you?" Had she been marked as a victim? Josie had long dark hair and the killer had been working her way down the alphabet with the first names of her victims. Was Josie on Regina Willard's radar for when she got to the letter *J*?

"I was a suspect in the case."

He stared at her for several long moments, wondering if perhaps he'd misheard what she'd just said. "A suspect?" he finally said. "Why on earth would the authorities think you might be the killer?"

Once again her gaze drifted to someplace just behind him and she shifted positions on the sofa, then released a deep sigh. "The red bull's-eye on the forehead was the same MO as another serial killer who was at work in and around Granite Gulch over twenty years ago. That man murdered nine men and one woman, my mother. His name is Matthew Colton. He's my father." This time when her gaze met his, her eyes were filled with a deep weariness.

A small wave of shock whispered through Tanner. He focused on keeping his features carefully schooled in neutrality. "I've worked here for the Coltons for years and never heard them mention your father or his crimes."

"I only met these Coltons for a brief moment, but

they don't strike me as the kind of people who would want to gossip about or ever acknowledge my father's existence," she replied ruefully. "In any case, I'm certainly not eager to have Sheriff Watkins find out about all of this with Eldridge missing. It will only confuse things for him because whatever happened to Eldridge has nothing to do with me or my father and what happened at that tree."

Tanner's brain worked overtime in an attempt to digest all the surprising information coming his way. "But the man in the woods…"

"That was definitely about me and my father." Her face paled once again. "It's true that my father is dying. He's in prison and is deathly ill. It's also true he requested to be buried with the watch that is supposedly here on the property. He said he wanted it for sentimental reasons, but my brothers and sister believe there is a possibility the watch contains a clue to money stashed someplace from old bank heists my father committed before he went away to prison."

"Apparently you and your siblings aren't the only ones who believe that," he replied. A chill tried to take hold of him as he thought about the moment the man had appeared with the gun. They had been lucky. Things could have gone so very wrong.

She leaned forward. "Tanner, I'm so sorry. The last thing I'd want to do is put you in any danger here." A strand of her hair fell over her shoulder and she quickly shoved it back behind her ear. "I desperately want that watch, still I'd leave in a hot minute to protect everyone here, but Sheriff Watkins has made that impossible. Right now more than anything I'm afraid for your safety. That man saw me with you and that puts you at risk as well as me."

"We'll both be safe around the house. After what happened to Eldridge, Whitney will see to it the security team is on top of their game. However, it's definitely too dangerous to try to dig up the watch again right now. It's even possible the man in the woods thinks you already have the watch. Are you sure you don't want to report this to the sheriff?"

"Positive." She sat back. "Besides, what could we tell him? I have no idea who the man was or where exactly he came from. I certainly don't know where he ran off to. I'd say Sheriff Watkins has enough on his plate right now without us adding to it. My oldest brother, Trevor, is an FBI agent. I'll let him know what's happened and he can work things from his end to see what he can find out about who else might want the watch."

Tanner was vaguely surprised to realize he was okay not reporting the incident to Sheriff Watkins. Normally he always tried to play by the rules, but in this particular case she made sense.

"I'll let the security team know to keep an eye out for any strangers lurking on the property, but I'm sure they're already doing that. And now we should get you settled into a room." He rose from the chair and she got up from the sofa.

"I have one bag to get out of my car," she said as they left his suite. "I only brought it in case it might take more than a day to find the watch."

It took only a few minutes to retrieve her bag from the car and have her move the vehicle to a parking area just outside of the staff wing. As they accomplished this, Tanner couldn't help but notice every cowboy in the area now wore their guns on their hips.

Whitney's son Zane, who was in charge of security on the ranch, would be tearing his hair out knowing somehow somebody had gotten to Eldridge in the master suite of the main house.

A quick phone call to Moira told Tanner two things—the room next to his suite was empty and everyone was still in virtual lockdown until further notice from the sheriff.

He now carried Josie's pink-flowered bag down the hallway to the small, empty staff room next to his. They hadn't even stepped inside the room when Brianna appeared pushing the stroller.

"Dada-love! Dada-love," the twins chanted with excitement at the sight of him.

Despite the happy greetings from his girls, his gut tightened at the pinched expression on Brianna's face. She stopped the stroller just in front of him and grabbed the end of her braid.

"How did lunch go?" he asked, wondering if perhaps one of the girls had misbehaved and that was the reason for Brianna's obvious unhappiness.

"They ate fine, they behaved okay, but I can't do this anymore," Brianna replied.

"Can't do what anymore?" he asked, even though he knew the answer and a heavy dread filled his chest.

"I can't work here anymore. There's just too much tension and I don't feel comfortable being here where a kidnapping took place. Everyone was up in arms in the staff dining room and I'm not sure my chakra is ever going to be right again."

The dread spread through his entire body. "So, are you giving me your two-week notice?" he asked as he set down Josie's suitcase on the carpeting.

"No, consider this your two-minute notice," she replied. "I need to get away from all the negative energy before I'm completely sick."

A wild panic took the place of the dread. Two-minute notice? What in the hell was he supposed to do with that? Before he could even respond Brianna raised her fingers in a familiar sign. "Peace out," she said and then twirled on her heels and headed back down the hall.

Tanner stared after her and then looked down at his daughters. "Dada-love?" Lily's lower lip began to tremble and Leigh echoed the cry.

He bent down and grabbed Lily into his arms, grateful when Josie picked up Leigh. He stared at the pretty young woman who held his daughter.

Josie had just confessed to him that she was not only the daughter of a serial killer, but had also been a suspect in a string of heinous murders, and yet as Leigh reached up to grab her nose, a crazy plan formulated in his head.

"How would you like a temporary nanny job?" he asked.

Her eyes widened in obvious surprise. "You're insane," she replied. Leigh laughed and clung tighter to her.

"It's too dangerous for us to go back to that tree for the watch for the next couple of days or so. You mentioned you mothered the other children when you were in foster care. If you'll play nanny to the girls during the day, then when I think it's safe enough I'll take you back to the tree to get the watch."

Her eyes narrowed. "That sounds suspiciously like blackmail," she said.

"Really? To me it sounded like the promise of a desperate father. Look, I'll pay you what I was paying Brianna and I'll start interviewing somebody for the position immediately. The girls have already taken to you and did I mention I'm desperate?"

"Nose," Leigh said and once again tried to capture Josie's nose.

Josie easily dodged the little fingers by turning her head slightly, but her gaze remained locked with his. "Okay," she said. "You just got yourself a temporary nanny."

Tanner should have felt a huge relief. He'd always considered himself a decent judge of character. But he'd certainly misjudged his former wife and then a couple of the women he'd hired to watch his girls. He just hoped he wasn't making another mistake in trusting Josie Colton with his most precious possessions.

Chapter 4

Josie stood and looked out the window from the small bedroom. Instead of getting settled into the guest room next to Tanner's suite, he'd shown her to the bedroom next to his with an adjoining door into the twins' nursery.

He'd given her the choice between the two rooms and she'd decided to take this one inside his suite. If she was going to play nanny to the two little girls, then she intended to do the job right and that meant being 100 percent available whenever they needed her. This room just made the most sense.

She didn't want to think about the fact that a lingering fear still coursed through her and it might have been that fear that had prompted her not to stay in the room next door all alone.

She placed her suitcase on the twin bed and quickly unpacked the few clothes she'd brought with her, then placed them in the chest of drawers. She'd packed for a couple nights' stay, not knowing what to expect when she got here.

She'd assumed she'd either be treated as a guest and given a room while she was here, or she might need to find a nearby motel to stay in until she could unearth the watch.

She set her toiletries aside for the time being. Tanner had told her to feel free to claim the guest bathroom across the hall from the nursery as her own.

He'd also told her to take her time getting settled in and she could officially start her nanny duties in the morning. At the moment he was entertaining his daughters in the living room.

She'd revealed a lot of her past to Tanner, but not all of it. She hadn't seen any reason to share with him the crime that had taken place so many years ago, a murder that had eventually forced her into the witness protection plan.

If things went the way they were supposed to, he'd never know about that part of her life. She shook her head ruefully. So far nothing had gone as she'd planned.

She finished unpacking her suitcase, pulled her cell phone from her purse and sat on the edge of the bed that was covered in a sunny yellow spread that matched the bright curtains hanging at the window.

She needed to call her brother Trevor. He would be expecting her to be back in Granite Gulch before nightfall, hopefully with the cursed watch in hand.

It had been only in the last month or so that she'd finally gotten the opportunity to get to know all of her siblings. They'd been separated first by the foster system and then by her fear of bringing danger into their lives.

Most of her siblings had gone into some form of law enforcement in an effort to protect their community from killers like their father. They worked hard to earn respect in the small town of Granite Gulch.

With a deep sigh, she punched the number that would connect her to Trevor. He answered on the second ring. "Are you already home?"

"Not even close," she replied. "We have a problem. Actually, we have several problems." She quickly told him about the missing Eldridge and Tanner and the man who had accosted them by the tree.

"Are you sure you're okay?" His deep voice held concern.

"I'm fine," she assured him, making an instant decision not to tell her big brother about the gunshot wound. "A little shaken up, but I'm okay. I just wanted to let you know Tanner thinks we shouldn't go back to dig up the watch for the next couple of days and I'm in lockdown here until the sheriff says

I can leave, so I'm not sure exactly when I'll be back home."

"Josie, the last thing any of us want is for you to get hurt. Take the time you need to assure you're safe. Now, tell me what this creep looks like."

She gave him a description of the gunman and he assured her he would do everything in his power to check out former cell mates and cohorts their father might have had in his years of incarceration.

When Josie finally ended the call she had no grandiose illusions that Trevor would manage to identify the man in the woods. There had been plenty of shady characters in her father's life. Dark dirty hair and a snarl weren't great details for Trevor to go on, but they were pretty much all she had.

She reminded herself that despite all the odds, Trevor and his pregnant wife had managed to take down the Alphabet Killer. They had put their own lives at risk, but had managed to get the vicious woman off the streets and into jail, where she belonged.

A smile curved Josie's lips as she thought of the ceremony she'd attended only the night before. Trevor and his wife, Jocelyn, had renewed their wedding vows and now Trevor was not only a real husband, but also a happy father-to-be.

She knew with certainty Trevor would be the kind of wonderful father the Colton children had never had in their lives. He and Jocelyn had a beautiful future before them and Josie couldn't be happier for her oldest brother.

Her smile fell away. Although Trevor had told her to be smart and play it safe, he'd also told her that Matthew's health was deteriorating a little more each day, adding a small ticking time bomb to the job of getting the watch to their father before he passed away.

She checked her watch and saw it was just a little before three. Tanner had told her before she'd begun to unpack that dinner was at five thirty and served in the staff dining room.

She kicked off her sandals, stretched out on the sun-kissed bedspread and closed her eyes. She'd gotten up early to make the drive here, and with the traumatic morning events a quick catnap sounded like a great idea.

Closing her eyes, she became aware of the high-pitched giggles of the little girls and Tanner's deeper, intensely pleasurable voice drifting back from the living room.

A nanny. Never in her wildest dreams had she ever considered a job taking care of children. The truth was she hadn't thought much about what kind of a job she wanted to get, although she needed to get one pretty quick.

Her nanny job was temporary, she reminded herself. Hopefully this new reality would exist for only a couple of days or so. She'd get the watch and then go back to Granite Gulch and figure out what she intended to do for the rest of her life.

Blood. There was so much blood. Mommy? Mommy, why is your dress so bloody? The shovel made funny noises as it bit into the hard Texas ground and Josie's mother stared up unseeing into the late afternoon sun.

Mommy? Mommy, wake up. Look, Mommy, there's a blue sky on the fence. Why is that funny writing on your forehead? Mommy? Please wake up and smile at me...

Josie came awake with a sharp gasp, for a moment disoriented as to where she was and what was happening. Her breath hitched in her chest as the horror of the nightmare completed its hold on her.

She remained still, allowing the gruesome visions from her sleep to fade as her breathing finally returned to normal. It hadn't been a crazy nightmare of strange images that made no sense, but it had been memories of the day her mother had been killed and buried by her father.

He'd shot her in the chest and then marked her forehead with a red bull's-eye. Josie had been with her father when he'd buried her next to a fence near the barn on the old family homestead.

Josie had often played by the old fence, and one day her mother had given her some paint. Josie had splashed blue color on it to make a pretty sky, and it had been that particular reclaimed memory that had solved the mystery as to where her father had buried her mother.

Matthew Colton had played a game with his children, forcing each one of them to visit him in prison, where he gave them clues as to where he'd buried his wife. His final clue had been "blue," and that had finally jolted loose the old memory in Josie.

It had taken her twenty years to access the memories and now they wouldn't leave her alone. She was haunted far too often by a three-year-old's perspective of that terrible day, when her father had dug a shallow grave for her mother near a fence with a splash of blue paint.

Her stomach growled and she sat up and looked at her watch. Almost five. Her catnap had been far longer than she had intended. Her tummy growled again to remind her that she'd missed lunch and had eaten only half an apple that morning for breakfast before she'd hit the road.

She got up from the bed and grabbed her toiletries and her purse, then headed out of the bedroom. She heard no noise from anyplace else in the suite as she went into the guest bathroom and closed the door behind her.

Her upper arm held a dull ache she hoped would be gone by morning. She didn't even want to think about the close call they'd had.

Sluicing cool water on her face in an effort to fully awaken and leave the dreams behind, she hoped the staff didn't dress up for dinner. She'd packed only a couple pairs of shorts and a few T-shirts along with a short, sleeveless nightgown.

"It is what it is," she muttered to her reflection in the mirror. A quick brush through her hair and a dab of lip gloss later, she left the bathroom and frowned at the silence. Had Tanner and the girls left?

She tossed her purse on her bed, then went back through the nursery, walked up the short hall and stepped into the living room. Tanner sat on the sofa thumbing through a magazine. He looked up at her.

"It's so quiet I thought maybe I was here by my-self," she said and sat in the chair opposite him. "Where are the girls?"

"Peggy, one of the maids, is doing me a favor. She took them for a walk and then she'll bring them back here and feed them dinner," he replied. "By that time we should be back from eating."

"Is she walking them outside?" Josie asked with a touch of alarm.

"No, she's just taking them down some hallways to give them a little bit of time out of the nursery."

"Do the girls eat dinner here rather than in the staff dining area?" she asked. "If I'm going on duty tomorrow, then I need to know what their usual schedule is."

He nodded, his blond hair glinting attractively in a shaft of sunlight that danced through the nearby win-dow. "They get up in the mornings around six thirty and eat breakfast here in the suite. They usually go down for a short morning nap around ten or so. Brianna always took them to the staff dining room for lunch and then they go down for an afternoon nap around two thirty. They eat dinner here in the suite and then it's bath- and bedtime around seven thirty."

"And what about your schedule as ranch foreman?" she asked.

"Up and out by six thirty or seven in the mornings and I'm usually back here in time to play with the girls for a little while before their bedtime. On Saturday and Sundays my days are considerably shorter." He cocked his head, his gaze curious. "What about you? What kind of work do you do back in Granite Gulch?"

"I'm between jobs at the moment," she replied. She wasn't prepared to tell him that she'd been out of witness protection for only a month and had yet to figure out what she wanted to do with the rest of her life. She'd worked as a waitress in Missouri while she'd finished up high school and then taken some college courses, but waitressing wasn't something she wanted to go back to. "Has there been any word on Eldridge while I was napping?"

"No, nothing that I've heard. If there is anything new we'll probably hear it at dinner." He glanced at his watch and stood. "We can head for the staff dining room. I know you didn't have a chance to eat lunch. You must be starving."

As she stood her stomach growled loud enough for him to hear. He grinned, a wonderful flash of straight white teeth and warmth. "Ah, yes. You are starving."

"Excuse me." She placed a hand over her rumbling belly as a wave of heat filled her cheeks.

"Come on. Let's get that noisy animal fed."

They exited the suite and once again wound through a labyrinth of hallways. "I don't suppose you want to leave bread crumbs for me so that I can find the staff dining room again," she asked ruefully. "This place is huge."

"All you have to remember is to take two rights and two lefts and you'll wind up in the kitchen area, where the staff dining room is located," he explained.

Josie's stomach rumbled yet again as the scent of tangy barbecue filled the air. "At least you won't starve while you're here," Tanner continued. "Bettina Morely, the head cook, makes magic when it comes to all kinds of food."

Tanner led her through double doors into a room with two long tables. There were already three women and two men seated at one of the tables and they were helping themselves to fill plates from the platters and bowls of food in the center of the table.

Their conversation halted at the sight of Josie and they all stared at her with unabashed curiosity. Tanner made the introductions and then he and Josie sat side by side.

"You picked a fine time to show up here," Linda,

one of the maids, said to Josie. "The whole house is in an uproar."

"So, I'm assuming there's no news about Eldridge's disappearance?" Tanner handed Josie a basket of large sandwich rolls.

"Oh, there's news and plenty of talk," Linda replied. She was a slightly plump middle-aged woman. Her brown eyes glittered brightly.

"Ms. Marceline came waltzing in while Sheriff Watkins was here and she refused to answer any of his questions. I heard she even told the sheriff to mind his own business. Nobody knows where she was all night. You know she's always hated her step-daddy."

Becky, another maid with strawberry blond hair, leaned back in her chair and shook her head. "And then there's the fact that Mr. Fowler had that big fight with Mr. Eldridge last night. It was definitely heated. Most of the staff and the family heard them yelling at each other."

"What was the fight about?" Tanner asked.

"The usual. He wanted his daddy to retire and name him CEO. They both screamed at each other. I'm surprised you didn't hear them all the way in your suite," Becky said.

"And don't forget Mrs. Whitney," Linda added. "I heard her alibi was she went into her private media room and watched a TV show and fell asleep with her earbuds in so she didn't hear anything." Linda rolled her eyes. "A little convenient, don't you think?"

"Sheriff Watkins is going to have his hands full with this investigation," Jeb, one of the ranch hands, replied.

Josie added pulled pork to her bun and it felt as if her brain crashed around in her head. She had a gunshot wound in her arm and a mission to accomplish. However, as she listened to the gossip shooting around the table, she realized this Colton clan was a pit of vipers, one of whom very possibly committed murder.

Tanner didn't approve of gossip, but he knew there was nothing he could do to halt the wild speculation that was like an extra side dish served up with the evening meal.

"Everyone knows Mr. Fowler wants his daddy to retire and name him CEO and chairman of the board of Colton Incorporated," Linda continued. "Last night wasn't the first time the two had fought about it." She looked at Tanner. "But that's not the biggest news of all. Did you hear Mitchell Flunt was taken into custody for more questioning?"

Tanner sat up straighter in his chair in stunned surprise. Mitchell Flunt was a groundskeeper who had been working for the Coltons for years. "Why?"

"Mitchell has been angry ever since he didn't get the big raise he asked for at the beginning of the year," Becky said. Her blue eyes grew wider. "And when Sheriff Watkins was interviewing him, he noticed Mitchell had some blood on his work boots.

Mitchell said the blood was his own, that he cut himself on a lawn-mower blade, but I guess the sheriff didn't believe his story. He took Mitchell right into custody."

"There was blood in the master suite," Linda said as if to remind everyone of the scene of the crime. "I heard there was tons of blood."

"Not tons," Tanner replied. "I saw it and there wasn't a lot." He frowned thoughtfully. "But what could Mitchell hope to gain by kidnapping or hurting Eldridge?"

"Might have just been a case of revenge," Becky said. "People do crazy things when they're angry, and Mitchell has been ticked off about that raise for months."

Tanner shook his head. "I just find it hard to believe Mitchell would do something like this because he didn't get a raise, especially when there are plenty of other people who might have a lot more to gain by Eldridge's death."

"It's going to be hard to know who might gain something from Mr. Eldridge's death," Linda said. "You two weren't around when Hugh Barrington showed up and told the sheriff that Mr. Eldridge left specific instructions, which he updated each year. His will is not to be opened until his death and not without a body. Mr. Barrington got all choked up about everything that's happened. He was practically sobbing like a baby when he talked to Sheriff Watkins."

Hugh Barrington had been Eldridge's attorney for

years and Tanner knew the two had shared a close friendship. He wasn't surprised Hugh was upset by Eldridge's disappearance.

Would the blood on Mitchell's boots prove to be Eldridge's? Or was the groundskeeper innocent and the culprit much closer to Eldridge? Would Eldridge be found someplace alive, or would his dead body turn up? Tanner certainly didn't envy Troy Watkins's job of solving the crime.

"Could you please pass me the potato salad?" Josie's voice suddenly reminded Tanner of her presence beside him.

He grabbed the large bowl in front of him and moved it to where she could serve herself. "I'm sorry. This hasn't exactly been pleasant dinner conversation for you."

"It's all right," she assured him with one of her gorgeous smiles. "I understand everyone is upset about what's happened."

Yes, everyone was upset, but there had also been a touch of glee among the merry maids with their gossip. There was no question the arrogant Fowler and snooty Marceline weren't favorites among the Colton staff.

Through the years there had also been a lot of speculation as to why an attractive woman like Whitney would marry a man over twenty years her senior. More than one member of the staff believed Whitney to be a gold digger who had married for money, not love.

"Surely we can find something better to talk about while we finish our meal," he said to everyone around the table.

"And we know your favorite topic of conversation is those little dolls of yours," Becky said with a smile. "Is Brianna still working out okay? She seemed a little unsettled earlier at lunch."

"Actually, she quit this afternoon, but Josie has agreed to act as temporary nanny until I can hire somebody else," Tanner replied.

"That's nice of you," Linda said with a speculative look at Josie.

"I'm stuck here until the sheriff tells me I can leave, so I figured I might as well help Tanner out," Josie replied easily.

"Where are the girls now?" Linda asked.

"With Peggy. You know she's always willing to step in when I need a little extra help." Tanner couldn't help but smile as he thought of the maid who was at least five years past retirement age, but still had a spring in her step and a twinkle in her eyes.

Peggy insisted she'd work for the Coltons until she died. Her husband had passed away three years ago and they'd had no children. Although officially she was still a maid, her time was mostly her own. She lived in one of the staff rooms down the hallway from Tanner and nobody required much work from her.

He relaxed a bit as the conversation remained on

the twins and then shifted to the hot weather that showed no sign of breaking.

"That was interesting," Josie said a half an hour later as the two of them walked back toward his suite.

"A healthy portion of gossip is always part of the staff meals," he replied.

"It just makes me wonder what gossip might be swirling around about me," she mused.

"You'll probably never know." Certainly he'd suspected that before his wife left him there had been plenty of rumors and speculation about him and the state of their marriage, even though he'd been oblivious to the truth.

"It doesn't matter to me. I learned to live with gossip a long time ago," she said.

As the daughter of a serial killer, he couldn't even begin to guess what she must have endured growing up. The fact that she seemed so well-adjusted only spoke of an inner strength he found admirable.

He also hadn't forgotten her sole concern after being shot had been for his safety and the welfare of his daughters. Josie Colton might have had a lot of bad breaks in her life, but she appeared to have a good heart. And she smelled like a wonderful dessert and fired more than just a little bit of lust inside him.

He paused with his hand on the doorknob to his suite. "Are you prepared for the chaos of an evening with the twins?"

"Bring it on." Her eyes shone with a warmth he found far too inviting.

He opened the door, hoping the girls' presence would tamp down the edge of desire that had unexpectedly welled up inside him.

"Dada-love, home!" Lily squealed from her seat in her high chair.

"Dada-love, home," Leigh echoed from the high chair next to her sister. Both of their mouths and bibs were smeared with red sauce from the spaghetti meal they were obviously enjoying.

Peggy smiled from her chair between the twins. Strands of her gray hair had sprung loose from the bun at the nape of her neck and a bit of spaghetti sauce clung to the front of her blue-flowered dress.

"You can always be sure of a grand reception when these two see you," she said.

Tanner smiled. "Hi, Lily-love. Hi, Leigh-love," he said as he touched the nose of each of the girls. "We'll see how long the good times last. I imagine when they're teenagers they won't always be so happy to see me."

Peggy got up from her chair and held out an arthritic gnarled hand to Josie. "I'm Peggy Albright, and I know you're Josie Colton and I understand you're going to be taking care of these two sweet peas for a while."

Josie gripped her hand and shook it. "It's nice to meet you, Peggy. Tanner has told me wonderful things about you."

A smile lit Peggy's wrinkled face. "Any man who loves his babies like Tanner does is a good man in my book." She looked at Josie. "They are sweet little girls and you should find them a real joy to be around."

"Thanks, Peggy, and I really appreciate you seeing to the girls this evening. I know it's past time for you to get some dinner." He looked at Leigh and Lily and then back to the old woman. "I think I can handle things from here."

Peggy nodded and started toward the door. "There's leftover spaghetti in the fridge and plenty of applesauce and green beans if they want more, but they both ate like little ranch hands. I think they're finished because they're playing with what's left on their plates instead of eating it."

"Hand," Lily said and held up a spaghetti-sauce-covered little hand.

"Spoon," Josie said and picked up the small spoon on Lily's tray and handed it to her. Lily laughed, turned to her sister and released a long string of babble. Leigh responded in kind and they both giggled like misbehaving schoolgirls.

Peggy laughed and shook her head, then said her goodbye and went out the door.

"So, which one do we hose off first?" Josie asked in good-natured humor.

A bubble of laughter rose to his lips. It surprised him. He rarely found laughter anymore unless it was at the antics of his daughters. "Maybe we should tag-team them. If you could wipe down Lily and I'll get Leigh?"

A few minutes later he and Josie were armed with warm washcloths and prepared to attend to the business of cleaning up the twins. "I'll just warn you— they hate to have their faces washed," Tanner said.

"No, Dada-love," Leigh said with a stern look as he approached her.

"We have to wash our faces so we can kiss Daddy," Josie said brightly.

"Kiss, Dada-love," Lily replied and raised her face to Josie's ministrations.

Leigh watched her sister then smiled up at Tanner. Tanner's heart exploded with love. He would do anything for his children. Since the day Helen had walked out on him—on them—Tanner had vowed his daughters would be his number one priority and he would fill their worlds with as much love and happiness as humanly possible.

He certainly had no desire to marry again; his life was full enough with his two girls. Besides, he'd failed miserably at marriage once, so he wasn't willing to try it again.

A half an hour later he and Josie sat on the living-room floor helping the girls build block towers. To be more precise, he and Josie built the tall towers and Leigh and Lily took great pleasure in knocking them down.

"Which one is older?" Josie set a blue block on top of his red one.

"Leigh. She's three minutes older than Lily," Tanner replied.

"Leigh," Lily said and threw her arms around her twin's neck. The two girls toppled over on their backs.

"No, Lee-lee," Leigh protested and struggled to get back to a sitting position.

"However, Lily is usually the ringleader if there's any trouble," Tanner said with an affectionate glance at the little girl in purple.

"Trouble," Lily echoed with a delightful grin.

Josie laughed, a musical sound Tanner found intensely attractive. "She's a bundle of trouble and she's proud of it. It's sweet how they call you 'Dada-love' each time they see you."

"I didn't realize how often I said it to them until one day they started saying it to me." He smiled at the girls. "At some point in time I'm going to have to break it to them that our last name isn't 'love.' But for now they're my Lily-love and my Leigh-love." The girls laughed and swatted yet another block tower down to the floor.

They remained on the living-room floor until just after seven, when Tanner got to his feet. "I'm going to get these two into the bathtub and ready for bed. Feel free to make yourself at home in here or relax in your room."

He needed a little distance from Josie. The last hour had been far too pleasant with her company. It almost felt as if they were a normal family and he knew better than to get caught up in that particular silly fantasy.

He'd learned from Helen that he wasn't man enough to make a woman happy. He didn't have what it took to be a life partner. However, even if he were in the market for a woman in his life, he knew with certainty it wouldn't be the very young, very beautiful Josie Colton.

By eight o'clock the twins were asleep and he went back into the living room, where Josie was curled up in the chair and staring out the window. Twilight was quickly turning into deepening night.

She appeared so small and oddly vulnerable as a small frown danced across her forehead.

"I hope you aren't thinking any dark thoughts," he said.

She turned to look at him and offered a small smile. "It's difficult not to have a few floating around in my head after the day we've had. Eldridge is still missing and someplace out there is a man with a gun who wants my father's watch."

"Everything is going to be okay." He had no way of knowing that, but he did have the need to reassure her and try to take away some of the darkness that filled her eyes. "In the next couple of days or so we'll manage to get that watch for you and Troy will release you and you'll be able to return to your home and family in Granite Gulch."

"And Eldridge will be found safe and sound and you'll hire an amazing new kind and loving nanny for your girls," she added and then stood. "And I think on that positive note, I'm going to call it a night."

"Then good night, Josie. I'll see you in the morning."

"Good night, Tanner. Sweet dreams."

He watched her until she disappeared from view and then he sat in the chair she had vacated and stared out the window. A deep exhaustion swept through him, one that wasn't physical but rather mental.

He'd been up most of the night before with Clementine in the barn. And this had been one hell of a long day. It felt like a lifetime ago he had gone into the parlor to tell Whitney a new foal had been born.

Although he was deeply worried about Eldridge's welfare, it was the thought of the gunman in the woods that concerned him at the moment.

How he wished he would have slammed the shovel over the man's head. If only he'd been six inches closer. If only he'd somehow managed to get to the gun before the man had retrieved it and run away.

He wanted his words to Josie to be true, that somehow she'd get what she needed without any harm coming to her, and he wanted Eldridge to be found safe.

As much as he wanted to relax a bit, he couldn't, not with the troubling thoughts that now filled his head. There was no question that there was the possibility of a murderer being inside the house and that was concerning enough, but now he worried about another one lurking around on the property outside of the house as well.

His safe, structured world suddenly felt fraught with danger.

Chapter 5

Josie awakened to the sound of childish gibbering and immediately jumped out of bed. Nanny duty, her brain registered. She quickly pulled on the same clothes she'd worn the day before and then hurried into the nursery.

"Good morning, Lily and Leigh," she said in greeting to the twins, who stood in their cribs and bounced with happiness at the sight of her.

She stepped up to Lily's crib. "I'll bet you two need a diaper change," she said and looked around for where the clean diapers might be kept.

"I thought I heard the chatter of little girls." Tanner appeared in the doorway clad in jeans and a navy T-shirt and smelling like minty soap, shaving cream and a faint hint of woodsy cologne.

The morning sun that danced through the room's window loved him, glinting in the golden strands of his hair and emphasizing the lean, sculptured lines of his face. Josie fought the impulse to reach up and rake her fingers through her own bed-head hair.

"I was just looking for the clean diapers," she said.

He walked over to the chest of drawers and opened the lower drawer. "Bottom drawer diapers, second from bottom is pajamas and the top two drawers are play clothes." He grabbed two of the disposable diapers and tossed her one.

"Did you sleep well?" he asked as he changed Leigh and she took care of Lily.

"I slept great. I was afraid my little nap yesterday would keep me awake all night, but I went right to sleep and I'm ready to face a new day with these two sweet munchkins." She picked up Lily in her arms and at the same time he finished diapering Leigh and grabbed her from her crib.

"I figured you'd already be gone by now," she said a moment later as she buckled Lily into her high chair. Coffee was already made in a pot on the countertop, letting her know he'd been awake for some time.

"I figured I could head out of here a little later today with it being your first day on the job. I thought I'd hang out to help you through breakfast and then I'll take off for work. Help yourself to the coffee."

"Thanks, and how about you pour yourself a cup and sit and relax while I show you I can do breakfast just fine on my own," she replied. "Right, girls? We can do this all by ourselves, can't we?" The twins grinned at her.

"Okay, if you insist," he replied.

"Eat!" Lily said and banged her palms on the high-chair tray.

"That's exactly what we're going to do," Josie replied. As Tanner poured himself a cup of coffee and then settled on a stool at the small island, she quickly toasted a piece of bread, buttered it and then cut it in half and gave each child a piece.

With them happily munching on the toast, she rummaged around in the cabinets and found a small skillet. It took her only another few minutes to gather what she needed from the refrigerator to make scrambled eggs with cheese.

"I'm assuming they don't have any allergies I need to worry about," she said, acutely aware of Tanner's gaze tracking her every movement.

"None that I'm aware of," he replied. "I'm already confident that I'm leaving them in good hands."

She turned to look at him and he offered her a warm smile. "And why is that?" she asked.

"First of all, you knew to put something in their hands immediately, and secondly, they have completely taken to you. I've always believed children and animals have an innate ability to recognize good people."

She turned back to the counter and began to whip the eggs and milk together. For years she'd been told she was a bad girl with a killer's blood running through her veins. "How did they act when the mean nanny was in control?"

"They fussed and cried more than usual. I thought maybe they were getting sick, but they were definitely reacting to the nanny. They are normally very happy girls and rarely cry without a good reason."

His deep love was evident in the softness of his tone. Josie couldn't help but wonder how different her own life might have been if she'd been raised by a doting, loving father and if her mother had lived.

She and her siblings would have all been raised together under one roof. Sure, there probably would have been fussing and fighting, but there also would have been a strong, familial bond between all of them.

What would it have been like if maybe her father would have taken her for an ice-cream cone or sat in the audience of a school play? What would it have felt like to see him beam with pride as she graduated from high school?

Lily and Leigh would know what it was like. There was no question in Josie's mind that Tanner would be there for all the big and small events in their lives. He was that kind of a man. He was that kind of a father.

It didn't take long for breakfast to be cooked and served up to the girls. Besides the cheesy scrambled eggs, she sliced up some strawberries and peeled an orange for them to share. Only when the girls were eating did she pour herself a cup of coffee and join Tanner at the island.

"Now, explain to me how dinner is going to work. You mentioned the girls usually ate here in the suite. Does that mean I should prepare dinner for us, too?"

"I obviously didn't think things through well enough when I told you their normal schedule. Usually Brianna fed the girls here and I went down to the staff dining room alone. When I came back here to the suite, Brianna left to go home."

"Then there's no reason we can't keep that same schedule. I'll eat dinner here with the girls and you can still go down to the staff dining room," she replied.

He shook his head. "No, we'll all eat dinner together in the dining room while you're here."

"I really don't mind doing it the way Brianna did it," she protested. "We can keep the same routine."

"I mind. Despite our little arrangement, you are supposed to be a guest here. Besides, I never wanted to eat with Brianna, but I'd like to have my evening meals with you and the girls."

To her surprise his cheeks grew a faint red and he quickly picked up his cup and stood.

"Then I'll fix lunch for the girls here in the suite," she replied.

"That sounds perfect. You probably saw the refrigerator is fully stocked and the pantry has plenty of canned goods. If you need anything at all you can talk to Bettina and she'll see that you have it.

And now I'd better get to work." He placed his cup in the sink and then walked over and kissed each of the girls on their foreheads. "Bye-bye. Daddy has to go to work now."

Lily and Leigh echoed his goodbye and waved with egg-covered fingers, and then he was gone. Josie refilled her coffee cup and returned to her stool at the island.

It was as if when he left more oxygen filled the room. Something about Tanner Grange definitely made her feel more than just a little bit breathless.

Breakfast and cleanup went off without a hitch. She dressed the girls for the day and then played with them on the floor in the nursery until they both showed signs of being ready for their morning naps.

Once they were asleep, she took a quick shower and then dressed in a pair of clean jean shorts and a red T-shirt advertising the café in Granite Gulch.

She tried to keep her mind empty but it didn't take long, as she sat in the chair in the living room with the silence surrounding her, for her head to fill with a hundred different thoughts.

It would be so easy to allow the twins to dig deep into her heart. Lily was a bundle of energy and more demanding than her shy sister, but both girls were wonderfully affectionate.

I'd like to have my evening meals with you and the girls.

Tanner's words teased in her mind. He'd been friendly and kind to her, but he certainly hadn't indicated to her that he felt the wild, crazy heart flutters around her that she felt whenever he was near.

You're a temporary nanny. You're here to unearth a buried watch and when that's done you'll be gone from here, she reminded herself. Her future, whatever that might be, was in Granite Gulch with the brothers and sister she was only now getting to know.

This wasn't the time to get involved with any man, whether it was a temporary fling or something more meaningful. She smiled inwardly. Still, there was no doubt if she was going to pick a man to have a hot fling with, Tanner would be at the top of the list.

At least with Tanner and the girls filling her thoughts she wasn't thinking about the armed man in the woods who had shot her in the arm.

Thankfully the wound didn't hurt so much today. She figured within another day or two she'd be able to take off the bandage. It could have been so much worse, she reminded herself.

A soft knock on the door sounded and she jumped out of the chair. Maybe it was Peggy checking in to make sure things were going all right. It had been obvious Peggy doted on the twins.

She opened the door to a woman she'd never seen before. Long blond hair framed an attractive face with pixie-like features. Sharp blue eyes gazed at Josie with open speculation.

"Hi, I'm Marceline Colton." She offered Josie a friendly smile. "I heard there was a new family member on the property and I thought I'd come by and introduce myself since we didn't get to meet yesterday. Is this a bad time?"

"The girls are down for a nap," Josie replied.

"Then my timing is perfect," Marceline said and swept past Josie and into the suite. She was clad in a pair of designer jeans that probably cost more than Josie's entire wardrobe and a pale blue blouse that hugged her slender waist. The scent of expensive perfume trailed behind her.

Josie's mind raced as she closed the door after the pretty young woman. Marceline was one of Whitney's daughters from a previous marriage and she was the one who had refused to answer any of Sheriff Watkins's questions the day before. According to the staff gossip, Marceline hated Eldridge. Josie thought she had it all straight in her head.

Marceline sat in the chair and Josie sank down on the edge of the sofa and eyed her warily, wondering what the woman was doing here.

"Don't look so worried. I'm not going to call you horrid names like my mother did. I know you're stuck here for the time being and I just thought you might need a friend while you're here." She smiled with what appeared to be genuine friendliness.

"How do you know about your mother calling me names?" Josie asked. "As I remember, you weren't there when it happened."

Marceline laughed. "Honey, if you cough in this house, by the time the staff and other family members finish reporting it to each other you'll hear that

you have a deadly case of pneumonia or tubercu-
losis."

Josie couldn't help but smile.

"Ah, good, you have a sense of humor. That makes
me like you already," Marceline said. "We're about
the same size except you're shorter than me. If you
need to borrow some clothes while you're stuck here,
don't hesitate to ask. I'd be glad to help you out."

"Thanks. That's very kind of you," Josie replied.

"You're hurt. What happened?" Marceline asked
and pointed to the bandage on Josie's arm.

"Oh, it's nothing. I'm a bit of a klutz and I ran into
the side of the counter and somehow cut myself." It
was lame, and Josie could only hope that nobody
in the house knew what had really happened in the
woods. The last thing she wanted was for her situation to add to the gossip.

"So, tell me about Josie Colton." Marceline leaned
back in the chair. "Are you married? Do you have
a boyfriend?"

"No, and no," Josie replied. "What about you?"

"No, and no," Marceline repeated with a grin.

For the next fifteen minutes the two women got
to know each other a little better. Josie talked about
her siblings and about being in foster care for years
and Marceline confessed she didn't get along well
with her siblings, especially her stepsister Alanna.

"Daddy Eldridge totally spoiled her," Marceline
said. "She's always acted like she was better than
all of us."

Josie heard the touch of jealousy in Marceline's voice as she continued to explain all the reasons she didn't like Alanna and half her other siblings.

Josie thought she heard the plaintive cry of a woman who felt largely ignored or disenfranchised by the rest of the family. Something about Marceline struck a chord of loneliness that Josie recognized well.

Their conversation was interrupted when the twins awakened and Marceline left so Josie could take care of her charges. As the girls ate a lunch of grilled cheese sandwiches and chicken noodle soup, Josie thought about the attractive woman who had come to visit.

She'd seemed nice enough, and even though they hadn't spent much time together, Josie had gotten the distinct feeling that Marceline was the one who might need a friend.

Josie wouldn't mind having a female friend while she was stuck here at the ranch. The fact that rumors swirled around Marceline and her relationship with Eldridge didn't particularly concern Josie.

After all, Josie knew better than most what it was like to have a finger of guilt pointed at her when she was completely innocent. Rumors meant nothing—only cold, hard facts were important.

The rest of the afternoon passed quickly as she enjoyed playing with the girls and eating an afternoon snack of crackers and fruit.

At just a little after four thirty she was seated on

the floor in the nursery with a twin on either side of her and a picture book open on her lap.

"Ball," she said and pointed to the bright red ball on one page.

"Ball," Lily replied and stabbed her chubby finger on the page.

"Leigh, can you say 'ball'?"

"Ball," Leigh echoed and smiled shyly and then leaned closer against Josie's side.

"Bunny," Josie said and pointed to the picture on the next page. The girls each repeated after her.

"Cat," Josie said.

"Cat," Tanner's deep voice replied.

Josie looked up to see him standing in the doorway as the girls greeted him with happy smiles. "Tanner, I didn't hear you come in. How long have you been there?"

"Long enough. Stay where you are," he said as Josie started to get up. "I'm going to take a quick shower. Daddy will be right back," he said to the girls and then disappeared from the doorway.

A moment later Josie heard water running and knew he was in the shower. A memory suddenly surfaced from the day before—Tanner stripping off his shirt for her to use to stanch the blood from her wound.

Muscled pecs, a taut abdomen and skin that looked imminently touchable. If she hadn't been in shock, if she hadn't been so afraid, she might have enjoyed the view much better. As it was, the memory of his bare chest was hot enough.

"Cat," Lily said, pulling Josie's thoughts out of the dangerous zone.

"Yes, that's a cat," Josie replied.

They had worked their way to a giraffe when Tanner reappeared, bent down and grabbed the twins. With his two little blond-haired girls riding on each hip, he smiled at Josie, who got to her feet.

"You look like you survived the day without any damage," he said.

"We had a great day," she replied. "They ate a good lunch and this afternoon we played all kinds of games. I even had a visitor while the girls took their morning naps."

"A visitor?" He raised a blond eyebrow in curiosity.

"Marceline stopped by. She introduced herself and told me she thought I might need a friend while I was here. She was very nice."

Tanner's eyebrows pulled together in a deep frown. "Don't trust her, Josie."

She looked at him in surprise. "I'm only going to be here a short time. If she wants to make nice with me, then I don't have a problem with that unless you don't want her in the suite."

"It's your decision, but I'm just warning you that Marceline has a reputation for being a snake in the grass. There's really only one person you can trust completely around here and that's me." His blue eyes held her gaze intently.

A wave of anxiety swept through Josie as she realized fully for the first time the only person she should truly trust while here was a very hot cowboy she'd known less than forty-eight hours.

Tanner wasn't happy about Marceline's visit to Josie. As he sat at the staff dining room table with the twins in their high chairs between him and Josie, he wondered what had prompted Marceline to make contact with Josie.

Certainly he didn't think it was as simple as Marceline wanting to be nice. Tanner would always believe Marceline's snootiness was part of what had eventually driven Helen away.

Nothing Marceline did was ever simple or straightforward. She always had an ulterior motive. So, what could she possibly want from Josie Colton? He wished he could figure it out.

As with the night before, the conversation swirling around the dinner table was gossip about Eldridge's disappearance and the interviews that Sheriff Watkins and his deputy sheriff, Charlie Kidwell, and Deputy Julie Clark had conducted that day.

It would take days, potentially weeks, for the sheriff and his team to interview all of the staff that made the ranch run like a well-oiled engine. There was a large number of household employees, but all of the outside workers as well. And as time ticked on, Tanner's fear for Eldridge grew deeper.

He couldn't do anything to solve that particular mystery, but he could do everything in his power to keep both his daughters and Josie safe and sound.

When he'd walked into the nursery and seen his girls happily engaged in reading a book with her, it had warmed his heart deeply. It was nothing short of amazing how quickly the twins had taken to her. He now glanced at the woman who was uppermost in his mind.

She was quiet, not getting involved in the speculation and rumors being batted around the table. Her attention was divided between the food on her plate and the twins.

How long would she be here? When would she want to attempt to find the watch again? How long before Sheriff Watkins told her she could return to Granite Gulch? It was strange that he'd known her for only a little over a day and already he knew he would miss her when she left.

He made himself a mental note to place an ad in the paper to advertise for a new nanny. God, how he dreaded a new search for somebody who could take care of his daughters with an abundance of affection and just the right kind of discipline. He'd learned by the last four nannies that what looked good on paper didn't necessarily translate to what he wanted for his girls.

"Some are saying that maybe Mrs. Whitney decided it was finally time to become a wealthy widow," Lorraine, one of the kitchen staff, said.

"And maybe she didn't want to wait around for nature to take its course," Linda added. "Mr. Eldridge was always at her to rein in her spending habits and her alibi isn't exactly rock-solid, since nobody I've heard from actually saw her sleeping in her media room."

"I'll bet she's already been burning up the internet with her online shopping," Lorraine replied. "You know, retail therapy…" Several of the other women at the table laughed.

"More," Lily said and pointed to the bowl of mashed potatoes in the center of the table.

"More, please," Josie said.

"More, pease," Lily replied with a proud smile.

"I'll get it," Tanner said and reached for the bowl to serve his daughter. Josie had been in charge of his daughters for only a single day but already he wished she'd stick around and continue working as his nanny. So far, she had all of the qualities he'd hoped for in a nanny.

But he knew better than to even ask her if she wanted a permanent position here with him. It was only because of a string of strange and troubling events that she had taken the job in the first place.

Even though she'd told him she was between jobs at the moment, she was far too young and too beautiful to want to spend her time holed up with two little ones on a ranch. This wasn't the life for somebody like her.

He was relieved when the meal was over and they could leave the dining room and the gossip behind and return to the suite. Minutes later he lifted the girls from their stroller and deposited them on the living-room floor as Josie sat cross-legged next to them.

"You know, you don't have to hang out in here with me and the girls in the evenings," he said. "You're free and aren't on duty once I'm here."

She smiled up at him. "I don't feel like I'm on duty and I enjoy spending time with you and the girls."

His heart squeezed tight in his chest. "I'm going to grab some toys. I'll be right back." He left the room and went into the nursery, where he retrieved a handful of the twins' favorite toys.

Was he so hungry for company that he'd feel good about any woman who said she enjoyed spending time with him? Or was there just something special about Josie Colton?

Playtime with the girls was always pleasant, but tonight it was especially fun. They played hide-and-seek, with Josie and the twins hiding first in his bathroom and then in her bedroom. When Tanner "found" them the two girls squealed and giggled with delight and raced around with unbridled excitement.

They built towers with the blocks and then played baby dolls, with the girls showing Josie how to feed the dolls from tiny little bottles. By the time seven o'clock came Leigh and Lily were rubbing their eyes and ready for their bath and bed.

"I think we wore them out," he said to Josie when he returned from putting the girls down for the night. "I don't believe they've ever gone to sleep so quickly."

She smiled. "They are so bright and beautiful, Tanner. You should be so proud of them."

"I am," he replied.

She got up from the floor and moved to sit in the chair. "You mentioned that you and your wife divorced before she was killed over a year ago. The girls must have been so young when you two split. Did the two of you share custody after the divorce?"

"Actually, when Helen walked out on me, she also walked out on the twins." A bad taste crept up in the back of his throat. The taste was of regrets and failure with more than a little touch of bitterness. "Would you like something to drink? Maybe a glass of wine or a beer?"

"I wouldn't say no to a glass of wine," she replied.

"White okay?"

"Perfect."

He poured her wine and then got himself a beer, his head still filled with thoughts of his marriage and the woman who had left him and their daughters behind without a second thought.

"Here you go," he said as he handed Josie the wineglass. He sat on the sofa and took a sip of his beer. "Helen lived in Dallas when I met her. She worked as a Realtor and was beautiful and charming and I was instantly all in with her. We had a crazy, whirlwind kind of romance and within six months we were married. She moved in here and when she got pregnant with the twins I thought life couldn't get any better. I didn't realize how unhappy she'd become."

He chased the new taste of self-recriminations down with another swallow of beer and then set the bottle on the coffee table in front of him.

"She didn't tell you she was unhappy?" Josie asked curiously.

He shook his head. "Oh, she had some complaints. She didn't like the way the Colton family treated her. She thought they were all mean and hateful. She was sometimes tired at night and I'd take over the care of the girls so she could go to bed early. But I thought they were just normal complaints and nothing serious. I didn't know how serious it was until the day she packed her bags to leave when the girls were almost five months old."

He paused a moment as the memories of that event raced through his mind. He'd come in from working in the barn to find Helen standing in the living room, two suitcases on the floor by her side.

She'd looked so beautiful in a blue blouse that enhanced the bright blue of her eyes. A pair of tailored slacks showcased her long, slender legs. Her blond hair had looked so shiny and her makeup had been perfect.

"I'm leaving," she'd said, her voice flat and cold.

He'd looked at her and then at her suitcases, unable to make sense of things. Leaving? He'd thought maybe she'd planned a weekend away with one of her old friends from Dallas, but it hadn't been as simple as a weekend jaunt.

He snapped his attention back to Josie. "She hated that I was a hired hand. She hated that the family members were so snotty to her and she felt as if they looked down on her and treated her badly because I was just part of the staff."

He hadn't ever talked to anyone about Helen, but now the words tumbled out of him as if released from a pressure cooker. "She told me I should have seen her unhappiness and that I never really listened to what she said. I was insensitive and dense. I guess I was because I never saw the end of my marriage coming. I thought everything was fine. I thought she loved being my wife and being a mother to the twins. Anyway, she moved in with a friend who had an apartment in Dallas and within two months we were officially divorced and a month after that she was killed in the car accident."

What he couldn't talk about—what he refused to speak aloud—was his deep and abiding anger toward Helen. He could understand if she wanted to divorce him, but he'd never, ever understand how easily she'd walked away from the babies she'd given birth to.

"And you've been beating yourself up ever since," Josie said softly.

He looked at her in surprise and then shrugged. "I was still so in love with her when she left and I guess I'm just sorry about the way things turned out. I wish things would have worked out differently. In any case, that was then and this is now."

For the next hour the conversation moved to the new gossip that had accompanied dinner and how Josie had spent the hours of the day with the twins.

"I wish I had a ranch of my own where the girls could have their own yard to play in. It would be nice for them to have a swing set or a sandbox," he said.

"Why haven't you bought yourself the ranch of your dreams?" Josie asked. "Is it a matter of finances?" She grimaced and offered him an apologetic smile. "I'm sorry. It's really none of my business."

"No, it's fine," he assured her. "And it isn't a matter of finances. It's more that I just haven't felt ready to take that next big leap in my life."

"As foreman, if you can be in charge of running a ranch this size, I'm sure you'd do fine on a ranch of your own," she replied.

He smiled at her. "Thanks for the vote of confidence. Eventually I'll make the move."

By nine o'clock the wine and the beer were long gone and Josie got up from the chair. "Morning comes early around here, so I think it's time I called it a night."

"That makes two of us." He got up from the sofa, and after murmured good-nights, she went into her bedroom. He turned off all the lights in the living room and went into his own room.

An hour later he lay on his back in bed and stared

up at the darkened ceiling. Usually the moment his head touched the pillow he fell asleep, but tonight sleep remained elusive.

Worry about Eldridge and Josie's armed stranger battled with memories of his shattered marriage and the guilt and anger he'd harbored in his heart since Helen's death.

If he'd been a better husband would she still be alive today? If he'd been a better man might he have been able to pick up the signs of his wife's huge discontent and done something about it? With time, would she have wanted to play an active role in her daughters' lives?

They were painful questions without answers and perhaps that was why they haunted him. Still, it had felt good to talk about it with Josie.

It had also felt good to talk a little bit about what kind of life he envisioned for himself and his daughters. His dream ranch wasn't anything huge or elaborate, and while he wanted it someday, he just wasn't ready to make that particular life change right now. Heck, his most imminent need right now was to find a new nanny.

He must have fallen asleep, for he jerked awake with hyperawareness. The illuminated numbers on his clock let him know it was just after two. Had one of the girls cried out for him? It didn't happen often, but occasionally it did.

A soft noise came from the living room. Definitely not the girls, who thankfully had yet to attempt to climb out of their cribs. Adrenaline flooded through him and he grabbed his gun from the nightstand and slid out from under the bedsheets.

He was aware that it might be Josie, but with everything going on around the ranch, he wasn't about to take any chances. Grasping the gun handle firmly, he crept down the short hall and into the living room.

He breathed a sigh of relief and lowered his gun. Josie stood in front of the refrigerator clad in a short gold nightgown. Thin spaghetti straps crossed her slender shoulders and her hair spilled down in slight disarray.

She grabbed a bottle of water from the shelf and then turned and squeaked in surprise. "Tanner, I'm so sorry. I was trying to be as quiet as possible. I—I had a nightmare that woke me up and I just wanted something to drink."

With the light of the refrigerator behind her and the thin material of the nightgown, she looked nearly naked. Her taut nipples appeared to seek his attention as they pressed against the gown and his mouth went completely dry.

He cleared his throat as she turned and closed the refrigerator door, then faced him once again. "It's okay. I'm a really light sleeper," he said. He had no idea if his reply actually made sense or not.

Brilliant moonlight splashed in the window. His brain flashed with a vision of her in his bed, her hair splayed across the pillow, her eyes glowing golden green as he kissed her, as he took full possession of her.

"Then I guess I'll just see you in the morning," she said and quickly raced past him and down the hallway to disappear into her bedroom.

He remained standing in place and attempted to tamp down the flames of want that had fired through his veins. At dinner he'd wished Josie could stick around for a long time. However, now with his inappropriate desire for her still rushing through him, he hoped she'd leave the ranch sooner rather than later.

Before he did something stupid.

Chapter 6

Desire.

It had shone from his blue eyes, bathing her in a white-hot fire that easily rivaled the hot July sun. She'd wanted to fall into Tanner's arms, allow him to lead her into his bedroom and act on the fiery want that his gaze had promised as it had lingered on her.

Josie now shifted positions in the chair and stared out of the nearby window. After running back into the bedroom it had taken her a very long time to go back to sleep.

The nightmare that had pulled her from her bed had been a familiar one. The encounter with Tanner in the kitchen had definitely not been familiar, but it had definitely excited her and made her wonder what the morning would bring.

Thankfully everything had been normal between them. Tanner had helped her with breakfast for the girls and it was as if that moment in the kitchen in the middle of the night had never happened.

But it had happened and now she couldn't get it out of her mind. It had teased her as the girls had taken their morning nap, it had replayed over and over again in her mind as she'd fed them lunch, and now they were down for their afternoon nap and it still filled her head.

He'd looked like a model for a hot gunslinger calendar clad in his sexy black boxers and nothing else except the gun in his hand. Drat the man anyway. Why couldn't he be paunchy and unattractive? And why did he have to be so nice, so wonderfully supportive of her? If he'd been a jerk then she wouldn't be sitting here thinking such inappropriate thoughts about him.

She got up from the chair and went to the refrigerator to get herself a glass of iced tea. She wasn't sure what to do with the crazy feelings Tanner stirred inside her. And they were crazy, considering the short time she'd known him. But she had to admit they felt crazy good.

She hadn't dated anyone while she'd been living in the small Missouri town and under protective custody. It had been too difficult to trust anyone. She'd been afraid to get involved with anyone.

But that didn't mean she didn't know what she wanted in a man. She'd had plenty of time to think about it since her brief young love when she'd been seventeen.

She returned to the chair and once again cast her gaze out the window. The view was of a tree-dotted lawn and large outbuildings in the distance. She recognized the barn where Tanner had grabbed the shovel and several more buildings that appeared to be barns as well. Her car was parked near the first barn, next to several other vehicles.

Sipping her tea, her thoughts turned to the conversation she and Tanner had shared the night before. She found it difficult to believe Tanner's marriage had fallen apart because he was insensitive, although she'd gotten the distinct impression he believed the failure of his marriage was entirely his fault.

He'd loved his wife when she'd left him, and Josie suspected he still loved her. She'd been the woman he'd chosen to spend the rest of his life with, the woman he'd wanted to mother his children and grow old with.

It certainly wasn't any of Josie's business, but the tragic ending of his ex-wife's life had left two little girls forever motherless and she found that particularly heartrending.

Tanner had mentioned that morning he was going to place an ad in the paper for a new nanny and Josie had offered to conduct the interviews for him.

He had a job to do and it would be easier for him

if she interviewed for the nanny position. Besides, she certainly knew what he wanted from a woman who would take care of his girls and she wanted the same thing for them. Josie would make sure when she left here the twins would be in good, loving and capable hands.

He apparently trusted her judgment, for he had agreed he'd like her to speak with anyone who applied for the position.

She couldn't help but wonder if Tanner would ever allow the love of another woman into his life. Had his marriage experience turned him completely off the possibility of another marriage?

He deserved to have a loving woman by his side. The girls deserved to have a woman who could love and raise them. Not just a nanny, but somebody they could call Mother.

She released a sigh. Tanner hadn't mentioned taking her back to the tree to dig up the watch. How long would it take before he believed it safe enough to try again? If Sheriff Watkins allowed her to leave tomorrow, could she just turn her back on her duty to retrieve the watch for her father? Could she turn her back on the twins knowing a nanny wasn't currently in place to take care of them?

She didn't know the answer. The last thing she wanted to do was return to Granite Gulch and tell her brothers and sister that she'd failed to do the one thing they'd asked her to do. She had waited so long to finally be reunited with them.

No, she didn't want to go home empty-handed, but she also didn't think she could leave Tanner in the lurch where his daughters were concerned.

Peggy obviously adored the girls, but Peggy wasn't exactly a spring chicken and Josie had a feeling more than an hour or two with the rambunctious and energy-filled twins would be too much for the woman.

She sat up straighter in the chair as a flash of movement in the distance caught her attention. Was somebody hiding behind the tree trunk? Was someone watching the suite? Watching her?

Every nerve in her body electrified. The wound in her arm pulsed painfully and her heart raced. Was it the man who had shot her? Or had a spark of the sunlight tricked her into thinking she'd seen somebody?

Goose bumps shivered up her back and over her arms as she continued to stare at the large tree in the distance. Memories from her time in witness protection shot through her.

Always watch your back. Somebody is coming for you, Josie. Danger might come out of nowhere at any moment. She'd lived with these feelings for almost seven long years.

She'd believed that painful part of her past was finally over, but she'd been wrong. The circumstances might be different, but there was still somebody out there who potentially wanted to harm her in order to get to her father's watch. The danger wasn't gone. It was very real and present.

"Up. Lily up!" the little voice called from the nursery.

There had been no more movement around the tree. *Maybe it was just your overactive imagination,* she thought and got up from the chair as Lily yelled for her again.

It would be nice to believe the man with the gun had not only run away from the scene in the woods, but had also left the entire area and crawled back into whatever hole he'd come from.

She hurried into the nursery, where the childish giggles and sweet sloppy kisses almost helped to banish the fear that had momentarily gripped her.

The scent of burned coffee lingered in the air, but couldn't quite compete with the hot burn of anxiety inside of Sheriff Troy Watkins's belly as he gazed down at the DNA results that had just come in.

Just as he had feared, the blood on the windowsill and the floor of the Colton master suite belonged to Eldridge. Troy had hoped it wouldn't be a match, but that hope had just died on the page of the report now on his desk in front of him.

Unfortunately, so far no further concrete evidence had turned up. The ground beneath the bedroom window had been too hard to allow any kind of footprint impression to be left behind. They had also been unable to lift any fingerprints from the window and sill. They had apparently been wiped clean.

Troy suspected all of the fingerprints in the bedroom that had been lifted would belong to Eldridge, Whitney and any member of the staff who had regular access to the room, but it would take time to match all the fingerprints with all of the people.

Time. It was passing all too quickly and in any case the more time that went by, the more difficult solving it would become.

He raised a hand and rubbed the center of his forehead, where a headache threatened to unleash with brain-crashing fury. Normally the problem in solving a crime was finding viable suspects. In this particular case the problem was that there were far too many suspects.

The more he'd questioned the Colton family and staff, the more motives had come to light. From disgruntled hired help to discontented sons and daughters and stepchildren, there was definitely no shortage of suspects in regard to whatever had happened to the billionaire baron.

One particular suspect was spending time in jail, but Troy knew he couldn't keep Mitchell Flunt behind bars for too much longer without charges being brought. And Troy didn't have enough solid evidence to present to the prosecuting attorney for any charges to be brought against Flunt.

Troy hoped the DNA results from the blood found on Flunt's boots would come in before the end of the day, otherwise Troy would have no choice but to release the man. And that didn't sit well with him.

He moved the DNA results aside and stared at the pile of reports of interviews that had been done. They were also in his computer, but Troy was old-school and still liked to actually hold a piece of paper in his hand and read it.

At the moment he didn't have to read anything to remember what was in the top interviews. Fowler Colton had attempted to downplay the fight he'd had with his father the night before the disappearance and Marceline had so far refused to cooperate at all.

And then there was Eldridge's beautiful, much younger wife's alibi. Whitney Colton had insisted she'd fallen asleep in her media room and had heard nothing that had happened in the bedroom. It was an alibi none of the staff or other family members had been able to substantiate.

Was it just an odd coincidence she just happened to be in another room on the night somebody had taken Eldridge from his bed? Or was it something far more ominous?

It certainly didn't help that one of the first things she'd done after the initial shock of her husband's disappearance had worn off was to contact the family attorney, Hugh Barrington, about Eldridge's will.

Forty-eight hours had passed and with each minute that ticked by Troy feared Eldridge's body would be found. If this was the work of one of his children or his wife for some sort of financial gain, then they hadn't known about the instructions Eldridge had left about his will not being opened without a body. But they all knew about it now.

So, was Eldridge dead or alive? There was no question in Troy's mind a crime had occurred. The blood and evidence in the bedroom indicated Eldridge hadn't left his bedroom under his own volition.

Thankfully so far the press hadn't gotten hold of the story. Troy had put the fear of a quick dismissal into the hearts of all the people who worked for him if they leaked anything at all about the case to any reporters.

He held no illusions that the press wouldn't eventually sniff out and report on Eldridge's mysterious disappearance and that could only complicate things. Bogus tips would start to come in, along with sightings of Eldridge everywhere from a chapel in Las Vegas to a fishing boat in the Florida swamps.

The headache Troy had been fighting all morning took hold. With another press of his hand against his forehead, he leaned back in his chair, closed his eyes and wondered what in the hell had happened to Eldridge Colton.

Tanner approached the pen inside the barn and watched the new foal move to hide behind her mother. "It's okay, little one. I'm not here to hurt you," he said softly. The foal eyed him warily and Clementine nickered as if telling her baby not to worry.

Leaning against the railing, Tanner checked his watch. Almost four. He could knock off for the day anytime, but for the first time since he'd started his job with the Coltons, he was reluctant to return to his suite.

Actually, the real problem was he couldn't wait to go to the suite and spend more time with Josie.

Josie… She'd filled his dreams after their brief meeting in the kitchen.

And those dreams had been unbelievably hot and erotic. He'd awakened fully aroused and only a long, cold morning shower had set him right. He'd felt like a fourteen-year-old kid with a body part he wasn't quite sure what to do with.

He was twelve years older than her, for crying out loud. She was far too young for him and completely off-limits. His mind certainly understood that, but apparently his body had no conscience.

He stepped back from the pen as Zane Colton walked into the barn. The muscular, dark-haired man, whom Eldridge had adopted soon after his marriage to Whitney, approached the pen and offered Tanner a smile that did little to lighten his dark eyes.

"Zane, how's it going?" Tanner asked.

Zane released a deep sigh. "I thought it was challenging to work head of security and deal with embezzlement and internet security issues, but that was nothing compared to what's happening around here now. I've hired on a couple of new men but it's too little too late for whatever happened to my father."

"Has anyone seen any strangers lurking around the ranch?" Tanner asked, thinking of the man he and Josie had encountered in the woods.

Zane shook his head. "Not that anyone has reported. My men are on high alert and are riding and walking the property, especially around the house. I don't want anything else to happen on my watch."

He leaned forward and rested his elbows on the top of the pen railing. He looked like a man with the weight of the world on his broad shoulders.

Tanner had always liked Zane and knew Eldridge's kidnapping had to weigh heavily on the young man's head. "Nobody saw this coming, Zane," he said softly. "Nobody could have predicted something like this happening."

"Yeah, I know." A hollow wind blew in Zane's voice and he was silent for a long moment. "I sure as hell wish I'd seen it coming so I could have stopped it before it happened."

"Monday-morning quarterbacking never helped anyone."

"Yeah, I know," he repeated. He straightened and met Tanner's gaze. "You know what really stinks?"

"What's that?"

"Not knowing who you can trust with the people who work for you. It especially stinks not knowing who to trust in your own family." He released a heavy sigh. "I'd better get back outside."

"And it's time for me to get inside and get cleaned up for dinner," Tanner replied, wishing there was something he could say to make the young man feel better. But at this point in time nothing short of finding Eldridge safe and sound could make anyone feel better.

"Your girls doing okay?" Zane asked as the two men headed for the barn exit.

"They're doing terrific."

"I heard Josie Colton is working as your nanny while she's here. How's that working out?" They left the barn and stepped out into the hot, late afternoon sun.

"She's terrific with the twins, but she's only going to be here a short time. Once Sheriff Watkins tells her she can go home, she'll be gone. I placed an ad in the paper this morning for a new nanny. Hopefully I can get somebody in place before Josie leaves to head back home."

"Good luck with that," Zane replied. The two bade their goodbyes and then Zane headed in the direction of the outbuilding where his office was located and Tanner walked toward the house.

It must be tough on Zane not even knowing if his own mother might be involved in whatever had happened to Eldridge, Tanner thought. There had always been more than a little rivalry and bickering among all the siblings, but this had to have taken it all to a whole new level.

Zane had said there had been no reports of strangers on the property. Maybe it would be safe enough to try to retrieve the watch again. And maybe if Josie spoke to Troy Watkins he would agree to allow her to return to Granite Gulch.

He didn't want her to go, but after last night he didn't trust himself with her. She not only posed an enormous temptation, but she'd also breathed a new life into his living quarters and had brought more laughter than ever before. Her exuberant youthfulness both tormented him and thoroughly charmed him.

He entered through the back door, where a member of the security team stood nearby. "Hey, John. How's it going?"

"Tense," the tall, thin man replied. "Everyone is on edge."

"I know. Even the cattle seemed restless when I rode among them this morning," Tanner replied. "Take it easy," he said and then went inside the building.

As Tanner wound his way toward his suite he steeled himself for being in Josie's presence once again. She was a pleasurable pain, a temptation he couldn't indulge in no matter how badly he wanted to.

She and the twins were in the nursery. Josie sat in one of the little chairs at the table, and Lily and Leigh were feeding her pretend food from a bright red plastic plate.

The twins ran to greet him and Josie's face wreathed into a welcoming smile he could get used to. "Ah, just in time," she said. "I've eaten enough ''sgetti' to last me a lifetime."

"'Sgetti!" Lily said and clapped her hands together.

Tanner laughed and gave each of his daughters a hug. "Daddy has to get cleaned up for dinner," he said. "I'll be ready in just a few minutes."

"Lily and Leigh, Josie wants more 'sgetti," Josie said as he left the nursery.

He took a quick shower and then changed into clean clothes and they all headed down to the dining room. Dinner was the usual affair. The roast beef and potatoes were served with a healthy dose of more gossip, including the fact that Mitchell Flunt had been charged with the possession of stolen goods and was awaiting arraignment.

"He had a saddle that belonged here on the ranch in his house and some other Colton equipment in his garage. I suppose he figured if he couldn't get a raise then he'd steal stuff and sell or pawn it," Linda said. "I never liked that man. He wasn't that friendly and he has beady little eyes."

Beady eyes or not, Tanner was surprised by this news. He wouldn't have pegged Flunt for a thief and there was still the question of the blood on Flunt's boots. Blood that had apparently been probable cause for Watkins to get a search warrant for Flunt's home.

If the blood on the work boots turned out not to belong to Eldridge, then it meant Troy would be looking harder at all the other people here on the ranch.

Thank God he had a solid alibi for the night Eldridge had gone missing and Josie had told him about her brother's vow renewal she'd attended in Granite Gulch the night before she'd arrived here. He had several other cowboys who could attest to where he had been and she had plenty of people who could substantiate her whereabouts for most of the night before Eldridge's kidnapping.

As far as he knew, nobody had pinned down the exact time Eldridge had gone missing. It could have been at any time after nine o'clock in the evening until just before he'd been discovered missing after eight the next morning.

Neither he nor Josie had anything to gain by kidnapping or killing Eldridge. Josie hadn't even met the man and everyone around the ranch knew Eldridge and Tanner shared a close relationship.

Josie had told him she hadn't wanted to tell Watkins anything about the watch or her background, but Tanner knew the sheriff would be thorough in his investigation and probably already knew Josie's father was the infamous serial killer Matthew Colton.

He now gazed over the twins' heads to where Josie was talking to Becky about a television show he'd never heard of. Josie's eyes sparkled with animation and he imagined he could smell her spicy, peachy fragrance despite the scents of cooked beef and vegetables that wafted in the air.

He barely had time to talk to her before they'd come down for the evening meal, but it was obvious the day had gone well with her and his girls.

He smiled as Lily offered him a bite of cooked carrot from her plate. "Lily-love, eat," he said softly.

"Dada-love, eat," she replied and held the bit of carrot between her fingers.

He leaned over and took the carrot from her with

his mouth and his gaze locked with Josie's. She gave him that warm, inviting smile that stoked a small, familiar flame in the pit of his stomach. God, the woman was excitingly dangerous and didn't even seem to know it.

"Now Lily-love, eat," he said and broke the eye contact with Josie.

The lyrics of an old jazz song suddenly played in his mind. *I got it bad, and that ain't good.* Oh, yes, he had it bad for Josie Colton and that definitely wasn't good.

She was like forbidden fruit, taboo to a jaded older man like him who hadn't even been smart enough to keep his wife happy. The worst thing he could do was entertain the thought of having any kind of romantic relationship with Josie.

All too quickly dinner was finished and it was time for them to return to the suite. He pushed the stroller and Josie walked beside him. Now for sure he could smell the fresh, sweet fruity scent of her that stirred him on all kinds of levels.

"That was the best pot roast I've ever tasted," she said.

"I told you Bettina was a great cook. Do you cook?"

"I'm definitely not chef quality, but I get by okay."

"Do you have a specialty?" He welcomed the banal conversation that kept his mind off more carnal thoughts.

"Chicken and dumplings," she replied without hesitation. "Maybe if I'm here long enough I'll make it for you and the girls one night. It would be nice to skip the gossip for a change and just focus on a good meal for the four of us."

"The gossip is definitely getting to be a little much," he agreed. "I won't believe anything unless I hear it from Troy's mouth or from one of his deputies." They reached the suite door and he unlocked it and they went inside.

"The ad for the new nanny will start running in tomorrow's paper," he said as he lifted each of the girls out of the stroller and put them on the living-room floor.

Josie immediately sat cross-legged on the carpeting and the twins fought for a space in her lap. "Hopefully somebody wonderful will apply for the job. You know I only want the best for them."

He nodded. Somebody wonderful was already on the job, Tanner thought, and his opinion didn't change in the next couple of hours as they entertained the twins with silly games of make-believe and indulged in small talk.

She was so easy to talk to and he was surprised to discover they shared not only the same common values, but also many of the same political views. There were some things they didn't agree on and a good-natured argument ensued.

"I'm telling you autumn is the very best time of the year," she now said.

He shook his head. "Spring, spring is the best.

The new grass comes in and everything smells fresh and green."

"And in the autumn you smell wood smoke and apples and crisp air," she countered. "You have hot cider and hayrides."

He laughed. "Excuse me if I don't get excited about hayrides. Working on a ranch, I have to lug around enough bales of hay to not want to see it in my leisure hours."

"Hay," Lily said and then shoved her baby doll into Tanner's lap.

Leigh followed Lily's lead and gave Josie her baby. "Hay," she repeated and the two laughed as if they shared a special joke.

"Two of my siblings are twins," she said. "My brother Christopher and my sister, Annabel, but they were raised in different foster homes."

Tanner looked at his girls. "I can't imagine the two of them being separated."

"They certainly seem to share a secret language between them," Josie replied. "I've heard that about twins."

"I think they use their secret language to make fun of all the adults," Tanner said wryly.

As if to prove his point, Lily looked at Leigh and chattered a lengthy string of what sounded like musical nonsense. Leigh looked at Tanner, then at Josie, and threw her head back and giggled.

"I think you're right," Josie said and then proceeded to tickle the girls until their sweet, infectious giggles were the only sound in the room.

Music. The laughter was music to Tanner's ears. Not just the giggling of his daughters, but also the sound of Josie's laughter filling the air.

It wasn't until the twins were in bed and the two of them were in the living room once again that he asked her about her day. "We didn't have much of a chance to talk before we went to dinner and I didn't ask this evening, but I'm assuming everything went smoothly today."

"The girls were terrific and everything was great."

They were the right words, but a faint frown scurried across her forehead and her eyes darkened. "But?" he asked with a touch of concern.

She leaned forward, her body radiating a tension he felt from across the room. "He's still out there, Tanner. The man in the woods is still out there. I saw him this afternoon hiding behind a tree. He's watching me and waiting."

Chapter 7

Tanner stood and turned toward the window. He pulled the shades closed and then returned to his chair and eyed her soberly. "Exactly when and where did you see him?"

Josie hated that the light and easy mood of the evening had transformed into something far darker. She hadn't even been sure she was going to tell him until the words had spilled from her mouth.

"This afternoon I was sitting where you are now when the girls were taking their nap. I got up to get myself something cold to drink and when I came back to the chair I looked outside and that's when I thought I saw somebody run and hide behind one of the tree trunks."

Her body reacted the same way it had in that moment. All of her muscles tensed and her heart raced wildly as a chill of fear gripped her heart. She wrapped her arms around herself and pressed farther back in the sofa cushion.

"What happened next?" he asked with a frown.

"Nothing. I watched the tree for several minutes but I didn't see him anymore and then the girls got up from their naps. I looked out the window several more times during the afternoon, but didn't see anything else that caused me any worry."

"And you're sure it was the same man from the woods?"

She stared at him for a long moment before replying. Had it been the same man? It had just been a flicker of movement in her peripheral vision. Had there even been a man there? Or had her mind played tricks on her?

She unwrapped her arms from around her shoulders and dropped her hands into her lap. She was suddenly sorry she'd even mentioned it. "I guess I'm not sure what I really saw," she finally admitted.

She drew in a deep breath and released it slowly. "I spent seven years looking over my shoulder, certain somebody was going to jump out of the woodwork and try to kill me. I guess it's possible I just had some sort of a flashback this afternoon and didn't see anyone outside trying to hide behind a tree."

She looked down at her hands, unable to hold his gaze as she confessed it might just have been a figment of her imagination. He probably thought she was crazy.

"Seven years of being afraid somebody was going to try to kill you? I don't understand..." His voice trailed off and she felt the weight of his intense gaze on her.

In her haste to explain her current mental state, she realized she'd inadvertently opened up a whole new can of worms. She drew in another deep breath and looked at him once again. "From the time I was seventeen until just a little over a month ago, I was in the witness protection plan."

His eyes widened. "Why?"

Her fingers locked together tightly in her lap as her mind cast her back in time, back to a place where terror had ruled her world.

"I told you I was raised in foster care. My foster parents, Roy and Rhonda Carlton, weren't bad people, but Roy's brother, Desmond, was a major drug lord. Roy and Rhonda were clueless about what Desmond was and just how evil he was."

Her fingers tightened around each other. "One night when I was twelve years old Roy and Rhonda decided to have a night out on the town and left Desmond to babysit all of us."

Funny how something that had happened over a decade ago could still cause her chest to tighten and make her heart beat to a frightening pace. Her fingers twisted together so tightly they turned white as the past rushed up to slam her in the face.

"We all went to bed as usual around eight thirty and it was around midnight when I woke up and wanted a drink of water." Her throat was suddenly as dry as it had been that night, when she'd awakened to the sound of voices in the living room.

She'd slipped out of the bunk bed, pleased she hadn't awakened any of the younger children who shared the room with her. She remembered she was clad in her favorite pink-flowered pajamas and exactly how the cool hardwood floor had felt beneath her bare feet.

"And so you got up to get a drink of water," Tanner said softly, prodding her to continue.

She jerked back to the here and now and nodded. "I got out of bed and I heard voices and I thought Roy and Rhonda had come home, but when I started to go into the living room Desmond was there with a man I'd never seen, and before I knew what was happening, Desmond stabbed him in the chest."

The horror of the brutality and the blood and the dead man falling backward to the floor suffused her. Once again she wrapped her arms around her shoulders in an attempt to stanch the cold wind that blew through her.

Run, a childish voice screamed in her head. *Run and don't let Desmond catch you. Don't let him see you.* But she hadn't run. She'd been frozen in place by a sheer terror she'd never felt before.

"He murdered him, Tanner. He killed him in cold blood. I thought I could just quietly run back down the hallway and Desmond would never know what I saw, but I must have gasped or something. Desmond grabbed me by the shoulders." Tanner faded away as she remembered Desmond's dark eyes glaring at her and the painful pinch of his fingers into her soft flesh.

Desmond's breath had been hot and sour in her face as he'd whispered harshly exactly what would happen to her if she ever told anyone about what she'd seen.

"Josie…stay with me." Tanner's deep voice pulled her out of the past and back into the present once again.

She flashed him a grateful smile that lasted only a moment and then fell away. "Desmond promised if I told anyone about what I saw he wouldn't kill me, but he'd kill everyone I loved, including Roy and Rhonda and all the kids in the house. He said he'd hunt down each and every one of my biological siblings and see to it that they all died a slow and painful death."

She released a shuddery sigh. "I believed him and so I didn't tell anyone for five long years. I isolated myself from everyone. I even refused to see my biological family members when they finally found me because I was terrified Desmond and his henchmen would follow through on his promise to kill them."

"What happened next?" Tanner held her gaze.

She shrugged. "I went back to bed. I heard more voices and I now realize they must have belonged to a couple of Desmond's men. Apparently they took the body out of the house and then there was silence until Roy and Rhonda came home."

She released another deep sigh. She'd been frozen

in the bed with the sheets pulled over her head as if that might stop the threat from reaching her. But nothing had stopped the cold, hard knowledge that Desmond's warning was very real.

"Over the next five years Desmond never let me forget his vow of death to everyone I loved if I told anyone about what he'd done. Anytime he was around, he reminded me with a dark gaze or with his tongue hanging out of the side of his mouth like he was a dead person, when nobody else was looking."

"But something must have changed. Eventually you did tell somebody," Tanner said.

She nodded. "Things changed when I fell in love. I was a sophomore in high school and Michaèl was a junior. I was really happy for the first time in my life. We dated in secret and on my seventeenth birthday he proposed to me and we made plans to marry just as soon as I graduated from high school. I really believed everything was going to be wonderful."

Michael had been a brilliant sun in the storm of her life. With the optimism of youth they'd loved each other and planned for a future together. God, they had been so young and so unbelievably naive.

She focused her gaze on Tanner once again. "And then I got home one night and Desmond was at the house and I realized I had no future with Michael or with anyone else as long as he had all the power. If Desmond knew I loved Michael, then Michael would be just one more target for Desmond's wrath."

To her surprise tears pressed hot behind her eyes

and her throat closed up with a wealth of emotion she'd never allowed herself to experience before. She gazed at Tanner helplessly, unable to speak without fear of breaking down altogether.

Tanner got up from the chair and walked over to sink down on the sofa next to her. He took one of her hands in his and squeezed it gently.

She swallowed several times in an attempt to gain control and finally she continued. "The next day I broke up with Michael and then I left school and walked to the nearest police station. I told a detective everything and thank God he believed me. What I didn't know was Desmond had been on their radar for years and I was the witness to a crime that could finally take him down."

"And all you had to do was give up your life." His eyes held a warmth that bathed her, that stole away the chill that had held her in its grip.

"I didn't have a choice," she said ruefully. "I knew I would never have a life if I didn't tell somebody. The man he had killed, Blake 'the Snake' Biltmore, was a small-time dealer who had apparently crossed Desmond. His body had been found two weeks after the murder but the police hadn't been able to solve the crime until I came forward." Tanner didn't release her hand and she was grateful for the warm contact.

"And so what happened? Was Desmond arrested?"

"No, the police tried to take him down in a sting operation and he was killed before he could ever be brought up on charges, but Desmond had plenty of henchmen who the police feared would come after me and so I was sent to live in a small town in Missouri."

"What changed that allowed you to finally leave the program?"

"The marshals in charge of my case believed all of the men who had worked for or with Desmond were gone. Some of them were killed on the streets by rival gang members and others died in prison. I was told there was nobody left for me to fear. It took seven long years but finally everyone believed it was safe, and I could be free."

"And do you believe you no longer have anything to fear from Desmond and his cohorts?" Tanner's piercing blue eyes seemed to be looking into her very soul.

"I want to believe it," she replied slowly. "I hope it's the truth, but that doesn't mean my brain might not have played a trick on me this afternoon when I thought I saw somebody hiding behind a tree. To be honest, when the man first jumped out at us in the woods, my initial thought was that one of Desmond's men had finally found me. I was sure he wanted revenge for me taking down Desmond's drug kingdom."

"But we know that isn't the case," he replied smoothly.

She released a small bitter laugh. "Right—I finally have the opportunity to build a life and now there's somebody else after me."

"Josie, you're safe here. We're safe as long as we

don't venture too far away from the house. I spoke to Zane Colton this afternoon. Remember I mentioned he's in charge of security here? He told me he's hired on some new people to assure the safety of everyone here at the ranch. As long as we stay away from that tree for a little while longer, you'll be just fine. And when the time comes to get the watch I'll be right by your side. You have nothing to worry about."

You'll be fine. You have nothing to worry about. His words washed over her with a sweetness that once again pulled tears to her eyes. Never in her life had anyone ever told her that she had nothing to worry about. Never in her life had she truly believed it as she did when she gazed into his eyes.

She started to thank him, but the words came out on a choked sob and suddenly she was crying like she'd never cried before in her life.

"Hey, hey," he exclaimed and immediately pulled her into his embrace with her head just beneath his chin. She turned her face into the clean scent of his shirt and continued to helplessly cry.

He cradled her against him, one hand stroking up and down her back. He didn't speak. He made no attempt to stop her tears. He simply held her while she cried for the lost years she'd experienced, years where there had been no real love, no caring, just the simple act of surviving and enduring.

For years she had kept her grief for her mother, for the death of her childhood and the loneliness of her life, in a tightly locked box. But now the box was open and all the emotions she'd ever stuffed inside spilled out in choking, messy tears.

Monsters came in all shapes and sizes. They came in the cotton scent of a father's shirt and in the flat, soulless eyes of a foster father's brother. Now there was a new monster, one with greasy hair and a killing greed shining from his eyes. She was so very tired of monsters.

Tanner's arms held her tight and it was easy for her to imagine he was a brave golden-haired monster slayer who had a magic that would keep her safe from any more monsters she might encounter.

The fanciful thought slowed her tears until finally they stopped. Still, she didn't move from his arms. For the first time in her life, at this single moment, she felt utterly safe and protected.

Slowly she became aware of the press of her breasts against the solid muscles of his chest. His scent, which was already so familiar, stole away the last of her grief and instead filled her with a new, far different emotion.

Slowly she raised her head and found her mouth mere inches from his. His eyes seemed to glaze and deepened to a midnight hue in color and she knew he was going to kiss her. And, oh, how she wanted him to.

His lips touched hers with a tentative, feather-like softness as if fearing their welcome. He had nothing to fear and to prove it to him she raised a hand to the back of his head and pressed her mouth firmly, openly, against his.

* * *

Her mouth was hot and demanding, and as their tongues battled in a fiery dance, Tanner had a fleeting thought that he'd officially lost his mind. However, as he tasted the heat and the utter sweetness of Josie's lips, he didn't want to find it.

It was impossible to think. He could only experience the heady wonder of actually kissing her. Her fingers played at the nape of his neck and created a teasing torment that made blood surge through him.

He'd hoped to offer her comfort, but now his desire for her was in complete control of him. He'd dreamed of kissing her, but even his wildest dreams hadn't lived up to the real-life experience.

Her petite curves fit neatly against him and he reached a hand up to stroke her hair. Soft and silky, just as he knew it would be. It was easy to imagine his fingers tangled in the strands as he thrust into her.

Her small moan cut through the hazy fog that had momentarily taken possession of his mind, and with a horrified gasp he broke the kiss, moved her aside and jumped up from the sofa.

He took two steps backward and stared at her, appalled by what had just happened, by his utter lack of self-control. "I'm so sorry," he said.

She gazed up at him, her eyes a warm golden green and her lips slightly plumped. "Sorry about what?"

"I shouldn't have kissed you." He jammed his hands into his pockets and rocked back on his heels, needing whatever distance from her he could get. All he really wanted to do was take her in his arms once again. "I'm sorry because it shouldn't have happened."

"But I wanted it to happen. Tanner, I'm very attracted to you."

The words washed over him in a combination of sweet warmth and cold dismay. "Josie, you shouldn't be attracted to me. I'm way too old for you."

"Age has nothing to do with attraction," she countered with a smile. "And I'm definitely not sorry we kissed. In fact, I'm hoping we will kiss again."

He pulled his hands from his pockets and took another step backward. She was killing him with her come-hither gaze and words of encouragement to continue the madness.

"It won't happen again, Josie. I think we both have enough serious issues going on in our lives. We don't need to mix in a relationship that will go nowhere and would only complicate things," he said firmly.

He hated how quickly her smile disappeared and the gold sparkle in her eyes faded, but somebody had to inject cold, hard reality into the crazy conversation.

And the cold, hard reality was that, despite his desire for her, he had no place in his life for a young woman like Josie. She would be a mistake and he wasn't willing to make that error again. There was no place for any woman in his life. "I think I'm going to call it a night," he said. "Good night, Josie."

"Good night, old man," she retorted with a touch of sarcasm.

He stiffened his shoulders and then turned and escaped into his bedroom, where the sight of her, the scent of her, was blessedly absent.

It took him forever to go to sleep and when he finally did he dreamed of Josie once again, her eyes gold and glittering with want as he stroked her soft skin and tasted her hot lips.

He awakened before dawn and dressed and left the suite before she or the girls were awake. He headed for the barn where his office was located. Once inside the small enclosure that held a desk, his work computer, a file cabinet and an ancient coffeemaker, he sat and thought about what had happened the night before.

He had been stunned and saddened by what she'd told him about her past. It was bad enough her mother had been murdered by her father when Josie was just a toddler. It was tragic that she and her siblings had been separated and forced into the foster-care system. But it was what she'd told him about Desmond that had broken his heart for her.

She'd been a twelve-year-old child who had seen a murder and had lived in terror for years. The father inside of him had wanted to find that little girl and somehow soothe her pain, even though logically he knew there was really nothing he could do to take away what she'd endured.

He couldn't imagine how alone she'd been for the

five years before she'd gone to the police and told them what she'd seen. To wake up with fear every morning and go to bed with it at night must have been horrifying for her. It had been a burden that would have completely broken most people. Still, she had survived it all.

That kiss.

That damnable kiss.

He reared back in his chair and frowned. What had he been thinking? He shook his head ruefully. The problem was he hadn't been thinking. He'd been driven by his own desire, acting on it without any rational thought. He couldn't allow it to happen again.

There was no way he believed her attraction to him was real. She'd told him she'd been out of witness protection for only a month. She'd spent most of her life isolated and afraid. They'd been thrown together due to exigent circumstances.

She was just focused in on him because he was probably the first male she'd interacted with in any meaningful way for a long time. She hadn't mentioned any other relationships other than the one she'd had when she'd been a teenager.

She was vulnerable, probably seeking some sort of connection now that she was out of the program and free to pursue a life. He knew he was decent-looking, but he still knew that any attraction she believed she felt for him had to be false.

Had she really seen somebody hiding behind a tree the day before? Had it been the man from the woods? She hadn't been sure, but if it hadn't just been her imagination, then it was still too soon for them to try to unearth the watch.

Time. They just needed more time and then hopefully one night they could sneak out and get what she'd come here for and then she could go back to Granite Gulch and build a life for herself.

She'd find some young man who didn't already have children, a man who would make her the entire center of his world. After all she had been through, she deserved that and so much more.

He was vaguely ashamed he'd run like a coward out of the suite before she'd awakened. He wasn't even sure what he'd been afraid would happen. Maybe he feared an awkwardness that would be unpleasant. But even having faced a gunman and delving back into her painful past, he had yet to see a trace of unpleasantness in her.

He needed her at the moment, and she needed him. He had to move past the kiss, past his desire for her, and keep things amiable and uncomplicated between them.

With this thought in mind, at noon he decided to check in with Josie and his girls. He walked into the suite to find the twins in their high chairs and Josie seated at the island. "Look, girls, Daddy-love is home for lunch," she said in obvious surprise.

He got peanut-butter-and-jelly kisses from Lily and Leigh and then joined Josie at the island. "You aren't eating?" he asked. She looked achingly beautiful in a bright pink sleeveless blouse tucked into a pair of denim shorts.

"I grabbed a sandwich while the girls were napping. Can I fix you something? Along with my awesome chicken and dumplings, I make a mean peanut-butter-and-jelly sandwich."

"No, thanks. I'm good." He was especially good given the fact that her tone was light and easy and it was as if last night and that very hot kiss had never happened.

"You were up and out of here early this morning," she said.

"Yeah, Thursdays are when I spend most of the morning in my office doing paperwork and ordering supplies. I always try to start the day extra early." He got up and went to the refrigerator and pulled out a bottle of water, aware he'd just told a little white lie. Although it was true that Thursdays were filled with paperwork and time in his office, he rarely left the suite before dawn like he had that morning.

"I didn't know you had an office."

He smiled. "Actually, *office* is too grand a word. It's just four wooden walls that make a small space in one of the barns, where I can do my official fore-man work. It's actually a pretty bleak area."

"Sounds like maybe you need some twin artwork to hang on the walls and make it more cheerful." She looked at the girls. "How about this afternoon we color pictures for Daddy-love?"

"Color!" Lily exclaimed and then popped a bite

of sliced banana into her mouth. Leigh nodded in eager agreement, her blond curls bouncing on top of her head.

"I'd never thought about hanging anything on the walls," Tanner admitted.

Josie smiled. "Just give us this afternoon and you'll have artwork to rival the greats."

"I can't think of anything I'd rather have than some pictures from my girls to look at when I'm working," he replied.

"What's your favorite color?" she asked.

"I guess I'm a blue kind of guy. What about you?"

"I'm definitely a pink kind of gal, although I'm getting very fond of purple." She looked at the girls and smiled. "Definitely pink and purple."

He saw the real affection that shone in her eyes as she gazed at the twins and it only made her more attractive to him. When she looked back at him the warmth was still in her gaze. "So, how are things around the ranch?"

"A bit tense," he admitted. "It's like nobody knows who they can trust anymore. It's hard not knowing if there's a killer in the house or on the grounds."

"There's only one person you can trust around here and that's me, cowboy," she replied with a teasing sparkle in her eyes. It was the same thing he'd told her and it somehow felt like a little secret they shared.

"And on that note, I'd better get back to work,"

he said. "I just figured I'd pop in here for a minute before I headed out to check things in the pastures."

"If you would have popped in twenty minutes ago you would have run into Marceline. She came by for another quick visit."

"You enjoyed her visit?" Tanner worked hard not to frown.

"I did, although our conversation was fairly superficial."

"Did she mention where she was on the night Eldridge disappeared?"

Josie shook her head, her dark hair gleaming in the sunlight from the window. "We talked about fashion and food and the only thing she said about Eldridge was that everyone is hoping for a ransom note or call. She seems a bit lonely to me. I was looking out the window not long after she left and saw her go into one of the barns."

"She was probably visiting her horse, Queenie. She loves to ride, and I'll admit she does take good care of her horse." Still, his instinct was to warn her again about Marceline, but he bit back the words.

He'd already told Josie not to trust the woman. But Josie was an adult and could form her own opinions. Besides, he didn't see how Marceline could really harm Josie.

He was just grateful that the kiss and the conversation afterward hadn't changed things between them. When he left the suite minutes later he was confident he and Josie were back on track.

As he headed to the stables to mount up and spend the afternoon in the pastures, he thought about the fact that a ransom demand for Eldridge hadn't been received yet.

Did the lack of a ransom mean the old man was dead? Or was he being held alive someplace and the kidnapper was just biding his time and hoping desperation would make for a bigger payoff?

And what in the hell was Marceline really doing visiting with Josie?

Chapter 8

The next week swept by quickly. Josie and Tanner and the twins fell into a comfortable routine that spun a happy fantasy in Josie's head.

She could easily imagine a life here with Tanner and his girls. They had started each morning sharing coffee while Lily and Leigh ate their breakfast, and then Tanner left for work.

In the evenings after eating with the rest of the staff they returned to the suite, where they played with the twins until their bedtime. Once the girls were asleep, she and Tanner spent a couple of hours just talking.

It was amazing to her that they didn't run out of things to talk about and that their conversations were so easy, so comfortable. It was as if she'd known him for months and each morning she looked forward to those hours with him at the end of the day.

The twins had definitely woven their way deep into her heart. They were wonderfully bright and funny and loving and she didn't like the idea of anyone else taking care of them.

And then there was Tanner. The kiss they'd shared had rocked her to her very core. Despite the fact that there had been no physical contact between them for the last week, a sharp yearning had simmered in the air between them.

She felt it and she knew he did, too. She saw it in the glitter of his eyes when he gazed at her and thought she wasn't looking. She felt his desire for her wafting from him when they were alone together in the living room and the twins were in the nursery sound asleep.

When she'd been in his arms, with his lips pressed against hers, it had felt so natural, so achingly right. She wanted more from him; she wanted him to make love to her. It had been in her mind every minute of every day since they'd shared that kiss.

The idea that he thought he was too old for her was laughable. He was only thirty-five, and besides, she was an old soul. She had no desire to spend her nights clubbing and dancing until dawn.

She wasn't an average twenty-three-year-old. She didn't want adventure or serial dating. She wanted stability and family. She wanted peace and she knew without a doubt she could find it here, with Tanner and the two girls who had won her heart.

She now stared out the window. The twins were down for their afternoon nap and the silence was far too conducive to thinking and spinning fantasies.

The last thing she wanted to think about was the watch. Over the past week she hadn't mentioned going to dig it up and neither had Tanner. If she looked deep inside she'd admit that the man in the woods had cast her back to a bad place and she hadn't quite pulled herself out of the darkness.

This place felt safe and she was reluctant to even think about leaving. Tanner felt safe, but other than wanting her physically, she had no idea how he really felt about her.

Certainly she was a convenience for him right now. There had been only one response so far to his ad for a new nanny and the woman hadn't even shown up for the interview.

It didn't help that Eldridge's kidnapping had made a big splash in the news. It wasn't every day a billionaire was taken right out of his own bedroom and the press had gone wild with the story.

Josie suspected the lack of responses to Tanner's ad had to do with nobody wanting to work at the Colton Valley Ranch right now. The house where a kidnapping had occurred wasn't exactly an attractive workplace.

A knock sounded at the door and Josie jumped up to answer. She opened the door and Marceline smiled at her and thrust out a vase with a bouquet of beautiful yellow roses.

"What's this?" Josie asked as she took the vase from her.

"Yellow roses are for friendship and I decided to bring them to you to brighten up your day." She swept past Josie and sank down on the sofa. "I guess the girls are napping?"

"They are, and thank you so much. These are beautiful." Josie placed the vase in the center of the island and then returned to her chair.

"I keep thinking one of these days I'll come in here and you'll be gone."

"If I had my way I might want to stay here forever," Josie replied.

"Really?" Marceline leaned forward, her eyes glittering brightly. "I just knew it. I thought I smelled a romance brewing around here. So, tell me, are you desperately, madly in love with Tanner?"

Josie laughed. "I don't know about love, but I definitely feel more than a little bit of healthy lust where he's concerned." It felt good to talk about her feelings with another female.

"And have you acted on that lust?"

"No, not really," Josie replied with a laugh and then sobered. "But I feel electrified whenever I'm around him. It's like all of my senses come alive in a way they never have before."

Marceline nodded. "It's a wonderful feeling, isn't it?"

Josie raised an eyebrow. "Tell me, Ms. Marceline, is there somebody who electrifies you?"

Marceline leaned back against the sofa cushion and laughed. "Heavens, no. I can only imagine what it must be like to feel that way about somebody."

"But you're so pretty. There must be plenty of men clamoring to get close to you."

"All the men I meet remind me of my stepbrother Fowler." Her upper lip curled up. "And he's such a pompous jerk. He's even gotten worse since Daddy Eldridge has disappeared."

"I'm sure you'll eventually find that special man who will make you happy for the rest of your life," Josie said.

"And I hope things work out between you and Tanner if that's what you want," she replied. She eyed Josie with open speculation. "You're so different from Helen."

"Really? How so?" Although it felt bad to gossip about a dead woman, Josie wouldn't mind knowing more about the woman who had captured Tanner's heart.

"Helen really wanted to be a Colton, not a Grange. She envied our money, our standing in society and everything else about us. I don't know if she was that way when she first married Tanner, or if she got that way living here with him."

"But she must have had good qualities for Tanner to have loved her," Josie replied.

"I'm sure she did, but to be honest, I didn't see many. Of course, I didn't spend much time around her, but when I did she just seemed rather unpleasant. And she was far more high-maintenance than you seem to be. She had to have her hair done and got her nails manicured regularly. She liked nice clothes and that's obviously not a priority with you."

Josie looked down at her T-shirt and shorts, wondering if she should be offended by Marceline's assessment. She decided not to be offended but was secretly rather amused. Her Colton roots were dirt poor and the only money any of them had was hard-earned, not inherited.

"I just can't imagine her walking away from those sweet baby girls," Josie confessed. "Maybe she was suffering some sort of depression."

"Maybe," Marceline said.

"I've only been here a little over a week and already I'm going to miss them desperately when I go back home."

"They are cute, aren't they? Do you want children?"

"Definitely. I'd love to have a big family," Josie replied. "What about you?"

"I don't know. Kids seem a little messy."

Josie laughed. "Oh, they are. They're messy and unpredictable and give the sloppiest kisses and they fill up your heart in a way nothing else will ever do."

"If you say so," Marceline replied dubiously.

"Up! Lily up," the little voice called from the nursery.

Marceline stood. "And that's my cue. I'll scoot on out of here and let you tend to the girls."

Josie got up from her chair. "Thank you so much

for the friendship roses, Marceline. That was so kind of you."

Marceline gave her a quick hug. "Thank you for letting me hang out here occasionally." With those words she was out the door and Josie hurried to the nursery.

It was an hour later when Tanner came in the door. He smelled of fresh air and sunshine and that hint of cologne she found so attractive.

The girls greeted him with hugs and kisses and then went back to playing with their toys.

"Good day?" Josie asked.

"Not bad," he replied and then frowned. "Where did the flowers come from?"

"Marceline brought them to me. She told me yellow roses are for friendship. They are the first roses I've ever gotten from anyone."

His brow smoothed out. "She's definitely playing nice with you."

"It's kind of nice to have a female friend to talk to. It's been a long time since I've had that in my life." She wasn't looking for pity. She was just stating a fact. While in witness protection she hadn't allowed anyone to get close to her. Even friends could mean potential danger.

Tanner's gaze held hers for a moment and then he moved toward his bedroom. "I'm just going to take a quick shower and change and then we can head to dinner."

"Sounds good to us, right, girls?"

As Tanner left the room, Josie thought about the frown that had creased his forehead when he'd seen the roses. Had he thought they might be from another man?

Tanner Grange definitely gave her mixed messages. He professed she was too young for him and he wasn't interested in her romantically, yet at times he looked at her as if she were his favorite dessert.

He certainly wasn't bringing her any flowers, but she'd gotten the distinct impression he wouldn't be pleased if some other man brought them to her. Definitely mixed messages.

She tried to tell herself that he was right—there was no future for her here no matter what fantasies she spun in her head. She'd known him for only ten days and ultimately her goal was to get the watch for her father and go back to Granite Gulch. But the idea of never seeing him, of never seeing his sweet babies again, already ached in her heart.

By the time he returned to the living room she had the girls in their stroller and they were ready to head to the staff dining room and the evening meal.

"Are you hungry?" he asked as they left the suite.

She grinned up at him. "When am I not? Actually, I was thinking that maybe this weekend I could make my chicken and dumplings for dinner one night."

"That sounds good to me," he replied easily.

"There's only one problem. I'm not sure where to get all the ingredients I need. I checked the refrigerator and pantry, and some ingredients are there, but I'm missing a few."

"Make a list and talk to Bettina in the kitchen. She'll hook you up with anything you need."

"How does Saturday night sound?"

"Saturday it is and I do expect the meal to live up to all the hype," he said teasingly.

A wave of warmth swept through her. It had just been in the past couple of days he'd started to tease her and she loved it. It spoke of the ease between them, of how comfortable they'd become with each other.

When they reached the dining room he grabbed Leigh and Josie got Lily from the stroller to deposit them in the awaiting high chairs.

They worked seamlessly together, buckling the belts and then tying on bibs. Again Josie was struck by how right, how natural it all felt. They were a perfect functioning team, just as two parents should be.

As always, the dinner experience was a slightly chaotic mix of passing serving bowls, eating and listening to the latest gossip. Thankfully the latter part was in short supply this evening. The sheriff and his people had stopped coming by the ranch, although Josie knew the investigation continued and they were continuing to interview people at the station.

The immediate concern for Eldridge's well-being had faded into an unspoken horrible resignation that he was probably dead. While the family members were supposedly still hoping for a ransom demand, after ten days Josie didn't think it was going to happen.

Tonight the gossip around the table was about a well-known movie star who had been caught in bed with her best friend's husband.

"I knew she was nothing but trash," Linda said. "She's always showing off her naked body parts in the movies."

"That doesn't make her trash," Becky protested. "She's just doing a job when she has a movie role."

"Getting into bed with your best friend's husband makes you trash," Linda exclaimed firmly.

"I don't know about trash, but it definitely shows you're missing a few morals," Josie added. "If you're married then you shouldn't cheat. If you feel like cheating then get a divorce. Marriage is supposed to mean something."

She straightened in her chair and warmth swept into her cheeks. "Sorry—I didn't mean to preach."

Linda laughed. "Honey, there's no need to apologize for speaking your mind. You spend most of these meals pretty quiet. It's nice to know you have opinions."

"Trust me, I have plenty of opinions," Josie replied with an easy grin.

"Just ask me," Tanner quipped, making everyone laugh.

The rest of the meal was pleasant as everyone expressed their opinions on topics ranging from politics to the best cut of beef.

Lily and Leigh behaved beautifully, earning them each an extra cookie for dessert. They started the walk back to the suite with Tanner and her arguing about what kind of cookie was the best in the world.

Tanner insisted it was oatmeal raisin and Josie rebutted with chocolate chip. "They're best just out of the oven, when the chips are warm and chocolaty goo."

"I've always had my chocolate chip cookies straight out of a store package," he replied. "Actually, I've always had all my cookies out of a package that I bought."

"That's tragic. So then I've just added my chocolate chip cookies to the menu for Saturday," she replied. "Chicken and dumplings and chocolate chip cookies—it will be a stellar meal to remember."

He laughed. "And we'll see if you make a believer out of me when it comes to what kind of cookie is best."

"Oh, trust me, Tanner. Sooner or later I do intend to make a believer out of you." And she wasn't just talking about cookies. She was talking about her... about them.

As they reached the suite, he opened the door and she pushed the stroller into the living room, where together they got the twins out to play until bedtime and he stored the stroller in a corner of his bedroom.

Lily grabbed the book Josie had been reading them before dinner, and as she held one side, Leigh grabbed the other. A tug-of-war ensued.

"Mine." Lily's face scrunched up in anger.

"No, Lee-lee," Leigh replied in protest. "Mine."

Josie stepped up and plucked the book from their hands. "If you can't share nice, then we don't play with the book."

Lily shoved Leigh and Leigh responded by pinching Lily's arm. Both girls wailed in outrage. Tanner grabbed Leigh up in his arms and walked with her to the chair and sat while Josie picked up Lily. Within seconds the tears had stopped.

"This is the first time I've seen them fight," Josie said.

"It doesn't happen often, but it happens," he replied.

Josie carried Lily to where Tanner was seated and bent down with the little girl in her arms. "You two are sisters," she said to the two. "Sisters don't fight. Sisters love each other. Lily loves Leigh and Leigh loves Lily."

Leigh leaned forward and wrapped her arms around her sister. "Love," she said. The two hugged each other and Josie looked up at Tanner.

He gazed at her with hot, hungry eyes and her heart fluttered wildly. Time stood still and it was only as Lily moved out of Josie's arms that he broke the eye contact. "Go play nice," he said to Leigh and set her back down on the floor.

"I'll just go get some more toys for them to play with." A wild heat filled Josie as she headed down the hallway to the nursery.

She wanted him to kiss her again. The energy in the air between them had crackled with the sexual energy that electrified her. She wanted him and she had no doubt in her mind that he wanted her, too.

She started past her bedroom door, but froze in her tracks as she glanced inside the room. Her heartbeat thundered at the sight of the drawers pulled out and emptied, and tossed on the floor. The bed was stripped down to the mattress and the window was open and missing the screen.

"Tanner," she cried in a strangled voice that she scarcely recognized as her own.

He appeared in the hallway. "Josie, what's wrong?"

She raised a trembling finger and pointed into her room. In three long strides he was at her side. A small gasp escaped him and he immediately threw his arm around her shoulder and led her back down the hall to the living room.

"Stay here," he said and then disappeared into his bedroom. He returned only moments later with his gun in his hand and a hard glaze in his eyes. "Let's get you and the girls into my bedroom. I've already cleared it and there's nobody in there."

He bent down and scooped up Lily in his arms. Josie got Leigh and they went into the bedroom, where he deposited Lily on the floor. "Stay in here and lock the door." There was a simmering urgency to his voice. He left the room and shut the door behind him.

* * *

"How in the hell did this happen?" Tanner turned to look at Zane. Both men stood in Josie's bedroom doorway. The first thing he had done after getting Josie and the twins safely in his bedroom was check the rest of the suite to make sure nobody was anywhere inside.

It wasn't just anger that now coursed through Tanner. He was also filled with a rich, dark fear. What if they'd been in the rooms when somebody had broken in? What if Josie had been sleeping in the bed? What if his babies had been in the nursery? The thoughts chilled him to the bone.

This was their home, a place that was supposed to be safe, not just for Josie, but for his girls as well. Now that sense of safety had been completely shattered. Somebody unwanted and unknown had violated the sanctity of his home.

"I've got security patrolling the house at regular intervals, but I don't have the resources to have every window and door covered twenty-four hours a day," Zane replied, his frustration evident in his strained tone. "I'm doing the best I can, Tanner."

"I know. I called Troy. He should be here soon," Tanner said. He'd also called Peggy to come and keep the twins occupied in his room while the sheriff investigated this newest crime. "Nobody has reported any strangers on the property?"

"No, but you know this is a big spread and my

men can't be everywhere." Zane frowned. "It was damn brazen of somebody to do this in the daylight."

"Thank God it didn't happen in the night," Tanner replied. At night they would have all been vulnerable with sleep. If this had happened at night it would have been a whole different scenario.

A knock sounded at the door. Tanner shoved his gun into his waistband and then answered it. Peggy gazed at him worriedly. He'd told her briefly on the phone that there had been a break-in. "Are the girls okay?" she asked.

"They're fine," he assured her. "They're in the bedroom with Josie. If you could watch them until after we're finished with things in here, I'd appreciate it. Sheriff Watkins should be arriving anytime now."

"I'll be glad to watch them." She went directly to the bedroom and a moment later Josie stepped out of the door.

Her pale face was pinched with tension and he wanted to pick her up in his arms and carry her away to a place where she was safe and fear didn't radiate from her eyes. There had already been far too much fear in her short life.

"Is the sheriff here yet?" she asked as her gaze shot down the hallway, where Zane still stood just outside of the bedroom door.

"I'm expecting him to arrive in the next few minutes or so," Tanner replied.

"It was the man in the woods. It has to have been him. That's the only thing that makes any sense. He believes I have the watch and so he broke in here to hunt for it." Her voice held a trace of breathlessness. "I knew he was watching us. I just knew it." Her hands clenched and unclenched at her sides. "He didn't go away. He's here and he did this."

"Nobody got hurt, Josie. We'll get through this," Tanner said in an effort to comfort her.

There was another knock at the door. "That should be Troy," he said and hurried to answer.

Troy entered, followed by Deputy Sheriff Charlie Kidwell and Deputy Julie Clark. "You called about a break-in?" Troy looked ten years older than he had when Tanner had last seen him.

"That's right," Tanner replied and then he and Josie led the three officers down the hallway, where Zane stepped out of the doorway to allow the sheriff and his team access.

Troy frowned at the mess in the room and then turned to look at Josie. "Have you checked to see if anything is missing?" he asked.

Josie shrugged. "I haven't been inside to check, but other than a credit card and some cash in my wallet in my purse, I really didn't come here with anything worth stealing."

"Go ahead and find your wallet, but try not to touch anything else," Troy instructed her.

Josie took two steps into the small room and then stepped across an overturned drawer. "Here's my purse. It's been emptied out." She bent down and picked up a hot-pink wallet from the floor and then rejoined them in the hallway.

She opened the wallet and then looked up at Troy. "It's all here—my driver's license, my credit card and the cash."

"So, this doesn't appear to be a random robbery," Troy stated.

"Looks like a search to me, boss," Charlie said.

"That's exactly what it was," Josie admitted. She glanced quickly at Tanner and then continued. "I think whoever broke in here was looking for my father's watch that I came here to dig up."

Troy looked at her for a long moment and then released a heavy sigh. "Why don't we go into the living room and you can tell me all about it. Charlie, check outside the building and see what you can find. Julie, see if you can lift some fingerprints in the room."

The three of them went back into the living room as the deputies got to work. Troy sat in the chair and Tanner sat next to Josie on the sofa.

He could feel the tension radiating off her and once again wanted to pull her into his embrace and tell her everything was going to be okay. But he couldn't do that and instead he settled for taking one of her icy cold hands into his.

"Now, tell me all about this watch," Troy said.

"It belongs to my father," Josie began.

"Matthew Colton," Troy stated flatly. Troy offered her a small smile. "Don't look so surprised that I know about your father. I do my homework."

Josie squeezed Tanner's hand and then explained to Troy about the watch and about the man who had accosted them in the woods.

Troy leaned forward and gave them both a hard look. "Let me get this straight. A man shot you in the woods? Why didn't you immediately report it?"

"It was on the morning Eldridge disappeared. Things were in chaos around here and we figured you already had your hands more than full," Tanner said.

"Besides, I'd never seen the man before in my life. I have no idea who he is and we could have only given you a general description," Josie added.

"And after I hit his hand with the shovel he turned tail and ran. We hoped he'd left the area," Tanner said.

"From what you've told me, I'd say it's obvious he didn't leave the area and he's probably the person who broke into the room." Troy pulled a notepad and pen from his pocket. "So give me whatever description of him that you have."

"Medium height and a little on the thin side," Josie said. "His hair was longish and filthy, but I'm not sure about his eye color." She looked at Tanner as if to confirm what she'd said.

He nodded. "Sounds right to me and his eyes were brown."

"And you'd never seen him before?" Troy held Josie's gaze intently.

"Never, but I'm assuming he followed me here

from Granite Gulch," she replied. "There were several times in the past couple of weeks I felt like I was being followed."

Troy wrote a few sentences and then shut his notebook and slid it back into his pocket. "Your family is well respected in Granite Gulch. Your brother Trevor is an FBI agent. Ridge is a search-and-rescue worker. Your brother Christopher is a private investigator and your sister, Annabel, is a rookie cop."

Tanner was surprised by how easily Troy rattled off the names and occupations of Josie's siblings. The lawman had definitely done his homework.

Josie nodded and raised her chin. "My sister and all of my brothers are good, solid citizens."

"And after checking extensively into your background, I've come to the conclusion that you are just like them. You're free to leave here whenever you want. I know where you live and will contact you if I have any more questions for you concerning our ongoing investigation."

She could leave. She was free to go. The words played over and over again in the back of Tanner's head as Troy and his people finished up.

Would she jump in her car first thing in the morning and go home? After tonight he wouldn't blame her for wanting to run from here.

He'd told himself that she was getting too close, that he was ready for her to leave, but now that she could drive away he realized how much he wasn't ready to tell her goodbye.

It was a little over two hours later when everyone else had finally left the suite and the twins were sleeping soundly in their cribs.

Zane had seen to it that a new screen was placed on Josie's bedroom window and had promised to up the security around the staff wing of the house, but Tanner didn't think the man would attempt a break-in again. He'd obviously been searching for the watch and hadn't found it in the room. There would be no reason for him to search the room again.

Troy had promised to get back in touch with them if he got a hit on any of the fingerprints Deputy Clark had managed to lift.

The fingerprint dust had been cleaned up and Tanner now picked up a drawer from the floor and returned it to the chest of drawers. "You know, Troy is probably right."

"Right about what?" Josie straightened from tucking in a clean top sheet on the bed.

"That the man who broke in here probably knew we'd be in the staff dining room. He didn't want a confrontation and he wasn't looking to hurt anyone."

"You won't convince me that when he jumped out from behind that tree in the woods he wasn't looking to hurt anyone," she said with darkened eyes. "But I agree. Tonight he just wanted the watch I don't have." She grabbed the pillow from the bed and stuffed it into a pillowcase.

At least some of the color had returned to her face, he thought as he picked up another drawer and slid it into place. Together they worked in silence to put the yellow spread back on the bed. It was only when the room was back in order that he gestured for her to go with him to the living room.

She curled up in one corner of the sofa and he went to the refrigerator and pulled out a beer for himself and poured her a glass of wine. He wasn't much of a drinker, but tonight was the first time in a long time he almost wished he had something stronger than beer to chase away the chill that remained in the pit of his stomach.

"Thanks," she said as he placed her glass on the coffee table.

He nodded and carried his beer bottle to the nearby chair. He set his gun on the end table, twisted off the bottle cap and took a long drink. "Now that Troy has said you can, are you going to leave?" His gut tightened as he waited for her reply.

She sighed. "Not yet. That is, unless you're ready to get rid of me."

"Not at all," he replied. He was positively schizophrenic where her presence here was concerned. He didn't want the temptation of her, but he really wasn't ready for her to leave him.

He didn't like the way she had filled up all the empty spaces in his life and yet he dreaded the empty spaces she would leave behind.

"I really don't want to leave you in a lurch with the girls and I also really don't want to go back to Granite Gulch without that watch in my hand."

"Tonight was just a grim reminder that we shouldn't go back to the tree right now. As you said, he's out there somewhere, and hopefully with more time and a plan, you and I could sneak away from here some night to get to the watch without him seeing us."

She leaned forward and picked up the glass of wine. She stared down into the liquid for a minute… two minutes.

When another long minute passed and she still hadn't spoken, still hadn't taken a drink, he called her name softly.

Slowly she raised her chin and he was stunned to see the glittering tears that chased themselves down her cheeks.

"I can't stop thinking about what might have happened if Lily and Leigh had been in the nursery. I can't believe how close danger came to them tonight." She placed the glass back on the coffee table without taking a drink.

"I should leave here. I should leave here now before anything bad happens to you or the girls." Her voice was a mere whisper.

His instinct was to get out of his chair, to go to her side and comfort her. But he remembered all too well the out-of-control kiss that had happened when he'd last attempted to comfort her.

Still, his gut clenched as he considered another real possibility. She could run from here, but the odds were that the man would follow her. As long as the man believed she had the watch in her possession, she was still at risk.

"Josie, that's the last thing you should do. I know it sounds crazy in light of what happened tonight, but you're probably safer here right now than anywhere else. Zane assured me that he was going to step up the patrols around here and he will. Hopefully Deputy Clark got some good fingerprints and the man who is after the watch can be identified and Troy can get him under arrest."

He sounded far more optimistic than he felt. He seriously doubted the intruder hadn't been smart enough to wear gloves, and the description they had given Watkins could fit a thousand men around the area.

Josie swiped away her tears and picked up the wineglass once again. She downed the contents in several large swallows and then set down the empty glass. "I'm just so tired of being afraid," she finally said. "I feel like I've spent my entire life being scared of something or somebody."

His heart squeezed tight with her pain. He tried to find the right words, but before he could speak again she stood. "I think it's time to call it a night. The last thing I want to do is sit around here and have a pity party."

He smiled at her. "Josie, I would never accuse you of being a woman who wallows in self-pity. I admire the inner strength I know you possess and I know that strength will get you through this. We're all going to get through this just fine."

She offered him a small smile in return. "When you say it, I almost believe it. Good night, Tanner. I'll see you in the morning."

Tanner remained in the chair long after Josie had disappeared from his view. He sipped the beer and replayed the events of the evening in his head. His initial fear was gone. The rage that had engulfed him because someone had broken in finally dissipated.

As long as they were all in the suite, nobody was going to harm them. Moving forward, his gun would never leave his side whether he was inside or out. If anyone wanted to hurt his girls or Josie, then they'd have to come through him.

What was left inside of him was a deep ache for Josie. She was filled with such life, such humor and charm despite a past that had been fraught with fear and insecurity.

He'd told her the truth. He believed right now she was safer here than if she went back to Granite Gulch. Here she was surrounded by a trained security team and she had him. In Granite Gulch he wasn't sure she really had anyone to watch her back twenty-four hours a day.

He finished his beer and grabbed the wineglass from the coffee table. He should be exhausted after the emotional roller-coaster ride of the night, but once he was in bed, sleep remained elusive.

Brilliant moonlight came in through his window

and the only sound was the faint rustle of the curtain moving from the air-conditioner vent just beneath it.

He tried to clear his mind but thoughts of Josie wouldn't leave him alone. When would Josie Colton get the right to be happy? If and when she finally managed to get the watch to her father, would her life then become safe? Was that the final act that needed to be accomplished to truly free her to find a sense of peace and lasting happiness?

He closed his eyes and drew in several deep, long breaths in an attempt to relax his body. Sleep was just about to claim him when he sensed he was no longer alone in the room. His eyes shot open and his hand reached for his gun.

"Tanner?" Her voice was a soft entreaty. "I can't sleep in that room tonight. Can I please sleep in here with you?"

Chapter 9

Josie didn't give him an opportunity to reply. She was afraid if she did he'd turn her away or get up and leave the room. And she not only needed to sleep in his bed, but she also needed his big and solid presence next to her.

She quickly walked around the king-size bed and slid in beneath the cotton sheets that held his heady scent.

"Okay?" she asked.

"Okay," he replied after a moment of hesitation. His voice sounded deeper than usual.

"I'm sorry, but even after all the cleanup in there, the room just felt tainted. Maybe I'll feel differently about it tomorrow night."

"It's okay, Josie. Just go to sleep."

He hadn't moved a muscle since she'd gotten into the bed and a thick tension wafted from him. She didn't want to go to sleep.

What she wanted was his strong arms to surround her. What she needed was his mouth on hers, taking the taste of fear away. She was certain of what she wanted, and she wanted Tanner to make love to her.

Since the night of their kiss they had been dancing around each other with a thick cloud of sexual want between them. Oh, yes, she knew exactly what she wanted, what she needed from him right now.

She moved closer to him on the mattress and turned on her side to face him. He lay on his back, his facial features visible in the spill of moonlight through the window.

His eyes were closed too tightly and a tic pulsed in his jawline. His lips pressed together in a taut slash, letting her know that sleep was the last thing on his mind.

She reached out her hand and placed it on his warm, muscled chest. "Tanner," she whispered. "I want you."

He turned his head to look at her and unadulterated desire flowed from his eyes. "Oh, Josie... I—I want you, too." The words sounded as if they were beaten out of the very depths of him.

"So, what are we going to do about it?" She moved her hand and felt the rapid beat of his heart beneath his warm skin.

"We shouldn't do anything about it." His glittering gaze held hers intently.

"But then we'd have regrets. Tanner." She caressed her hand across the width of his chest. "I've had enough regrets in my life. I don't want to live with any more."

With a low-throttled groan he turned over on his side and took her into his arms. He rolled her over on her back and then his mouth was on hers.

Hot and hungry, his lips demanded a response and she gladly gave it. She opened her mouth and their tongues swirled together. His hands caressed up and down her back and the heat of his touch radiated through the thin material of her nightgown.

It was exactly what she'd wanted—to taste his unbridled desire for her, to allow her desire for him to explode into something bigger than a man in the woods and something better than an intruder in the suite.

He tasted of the promise of things she'd never had in her life before. Of safety and passion and love. And he tasted of the man she wanted in her life forever.

"Josie, sweet Josie," he murmured as his lips moved from her mouth and slid down the column of her neck.

The sound of her name on his lips was sweet music. She wound her arms around him, loving the weight of him on top of her and the warmth of his body so intimately against her own. One of his hands moved from her back and slowly caressed up her stomach, up to cover one of her breasts.

Her nipple hardened through the material, as if eager for his touch, and her heartbeat quickened as his mouth crashed down on hers once again.

The kiss lasted only a moment before she wanted more. She gently nudged him aside and then sat up and pulled the nightgown over her head, leaving her clad only in a pair of silk panties.

"You're so beautiful." His husky voice shot a thrill through her, a thrill that intensified as he lifted her up to straddle him.

His slightly calloused palms covered her breasts and her hair fell over her shoulders as she leaned forward. His fingers toyed with the tips of her breasts and then he reared up so he could reach them with his mouth.

Once again she wrapped her arms around the back of his neck as he flicked his tongue and sucked on first one turgid tip and then the other.

Electric sensations shot through her, along with a rivulet of heat that stoked her need for him even higher. She rolled off the top of him but knelt beside him.

His eyes glittered like those of a wild animal. He was so beautiful. The moonlight loved the angles and planes of his face and his gorgeous body.

She kissed the center of his chest and then trailed lingering kisses down the length of his torso. When she reached the waistband of his boxers she raised her head and gazed at him expectantly.

In an instant the boxers were gone and she took

his velvety hardness into her mouth. He moaned and tangled his fingers into her hair as she moved her mouth up and down the length of him in an effort to give him the most pleasure.

"Josie…"

She raised her head and he rolled her over on her back. "Getting is good, but giving is just as good."

Shivers danced on her skin as he lowered his lips to her stomach and then worked his way down. She raised her hips to aid him as he removed her panties.

When he reached her sensitive center he used his tongue and his finger, and within seconds waves of pleasure crashed through her, over her.

She gasped his name and before the last shudder had left her body he positioned himself between her thighs and entered her. For a long moment neither of them moved. He filled her and it was as if their bodies had been made for each other.

Then he drew back his hips and thrust into her again. New exquisite sensations forced a moan from her. She was lost in him and she never, ever wanted to be found.

She arched her hips to meet each of his thrusts. Faster and faster they moved in a frenzy of need until they were both gasping.

"Tanner," she cried, shocked to feel the rising tension of another climax. It washed over her and at the same time he found his release, stiffening against her with another deep groan of pleasure.

He covered her mouth in a kiss that wasn't only a

fitting end to what they'd just shared, but also sealed him into her heart forever. A rush of emotions shot through her, bringing the burn of tears to her eyes.

Almost immediately he rose, grabbed his boxers from the floor and then without a word disappeared into the nearby bathroom. Josie rolled over on her back and stared up at the ceiling.

Love. It thundered in her heart and warmed her very soul. She'd spent all the years in witness protection dreaming of everything she wanted in her life. She'd only been able to imagine what love might feel like and now she knew.

Her heart sang with it and her soul was filled with a warmth that had nothing to do with the sexual connection they had just shared. This was a mind, body and soul warmth that came from loving a man to distraction.

She'd only dreamed of a man like Tanner and it was a kind and good fate who had delivered him to her. He had all the qualities she could ever want in a man. And Lily and Leigh were special bonuses to fill her heart completely.

She'd wondered what her future held and now she knew exactly what she wanted. She belonged here with Tanner and his two daughters. She wanted to be Tanner's wife and the mother to his children.

This was where her happiness lay—in Tanner's bed, in his life, in his heart. She could only hope he felt the same way about her.

She would get the cursed watch and take it back

to Granite Gulch. She'd fulfill her obligations to her father and then she would return here to truly start her happily-ever-after.

Although she would miss being close to her family in Granite Gulch, at least it was close enough that she and Tanner and the girls could visit her newfound siblings as often as they wanted.

Whoa! Slow down, girl, a voice shouted in her head. Her emotions were leaping way ahead of reality. It was way too soon for her to feel so strongly about Tanner. She didn't even know how Tanner felt about her. Oh, she knew he desired her, but that was a long way from the happily-ever-after she envisioned.

He came out of the bathroom clad once again in his boxers. He slid back in beneath the sheets and Josie immediately moved closer to his side.

With a sigh he placed an arm around her and she snuggled into him. She'd never felt so safe, so happy and so loved as she did with his warm body against hers, with his breath stirring the errant strands of her hair.

"No regrets," she said softly.

He tightened his arm around her. "Go to sleep, Josie."

And she did.

Regrets.

Tanner had awakened well before dawn. He'd been spooned around Josie's naked back with his arm thrown around her waist. Her curves had fit perfectly against his body and the scent of spicy peaches had filled his head, along with a million regrets.

He now sat on the back of his horse, Beau, and waved to several other cowboys who were on horseback in the distance. Although his first instinct that morning when he crawled out of bed had been to get out of the suite before Josie awoke, he'd stuck around to help her with breakfast.

She'd been in high spirits, teasing the girls and him. The brilliant sparkle in her eyes had cut through his heart. The gazes she'd cast toward him had been as if the two of them shared a special secret, one she was more than willing to repeat.

Making love to her had been like nothing he'd ever experienced before, even in his years of marriage. She'd been so giving, so utterly alive in his arms. She'd made him feel as if he were the strongest man and the best lover in the entire world.

Still, his head and his heart were filled with regrets. Hell, they hadn't even used any protection. How irresponsible was that? He'd acted like a hormone-driven teenager with no rational thought in his head.

He should have never allowed it to happen. He should have never let her come into his bed. At the very least he should have let her have the bed and he should have slept on the living-room sofa. Should have, could have—how many things he wished he'd done differently now that he was in the reality of day.

He flicked the reins and decided what he needed was a good, fast horseback ride to blow out the cobwebs in his brain before he went back to the suite for lunch. He'd made the mistake of agreeing to have lunch with Josie and his girls before he'd left that morning.

He turned Beau around and then gave him free rein. The powerful horse responded with a surge forward. The noon sun was hot, as was the slight breeze that slapped him in the face as Beau ran full out toward the stable.

The familiar scents of cattle and grass filled his head, thankfully momentarily chasing away the memory of spicy peaches and a warm woman.

As he passed the large hay barn, he caught a glimpse of Marceline coming out of one of the side doors. He frowned. What was she doing in that barn?

The question chased him to the stables, where he quickly cooled down Beau and returned the horse to his stall. It weighed heavy on his mind as he headed to the house. What on earth would Marceline Colton be doing in that particular barn? She'd looked almost furtive as she'd gazed around and then had quickly scurried away from the structure.

At the door to the house wing, an armed man stood with narrowed eyes and a tense posture. "Who are you?" Tanner asked, having never seen the man before. He dropped his hand to the butt of his gun.

"Gary Benton," he replied. "And who are you?"

"Tanner Grange, the ranch foreman. Who hired you?" Tanner asked.

"Zane Colton. I was hired on this morning."

Tanner eyed the man for a long moment and then nodded. "Good to have you on the job."

As Tanner went into the door, he made a mental note to himself. He wanted Zane to give him all the names of the new hires working security.

There were now far too many new men—strangers—on the property. With the new faces it would be difficult for anyone to know if Josie's gunman was among them.

He entered the suite to find the twins in their high chairs and Josie standing in front of the stove. "Great, you're just in time for mac and cheese and chicken bites. I'm getting ready to plate it now."

"Then my timing is perfect," he replied and then walked over to kiss his daughters. As always, they greeted him as if he were Santa Claus with a whole big bag of toys. But all he had were kisses and hugs, and thankfully they were still young enough to be happy with that.

"Can I do anything to help?" he asked as he eased down on one of the stools at the island.

She flashed him one of her bright smiles. "Nah, I've got this. Just sit and relax."

He watched as she served the girls on their little plastic plates and then she fixed him a plate and set it in front of him.

"Aren't you eating?" he asked as she sat on the stool next to him.

She grinned at him. "You always ask me that when you're here at lunchtime. I made myself an omelet when the girls were down for their morning nap. I'll eat again at dinnertime. By the way, we all took a trip to the kitchen a little while ago and I got all the ingredients I need for chicken and dumplings tomorrow night. Bettina hooked me up even though Fowler was in the kitchen throwing a fit about last night's dinner."

He looked at her in surprise. "Really? What was he upset about?"

"Apparently beef Wellington was on the menu last night and Fowler doesn't like it. Bettina told him it was what Whitney had wanted for dinner, but Fowler said he was now the man of the house and would be making all the decisions about meals and everything else. I have to admit, he sounded like a snotty little brat."

"He is a snotty little brat, but the real question is if he's a murderer as well," Tanner replied. "We both know he's on the top of the suspect list." Along with Marceline, he thought.

"Eat up before it gets cold," Josie said.

As he ate Josie filled him in on what she and the twins had done throughout the morning. It was difficult to remember that only the night before these rooms had been filled with the darkness of the break-in.

It was difficult not to remember that last night she'd been naked in his arms and their lovemaking had exceeded every fantasy and hot dream he'd had about her.

Thankfully she didn't seem to have any desire to rehash what had happened between them the night before. The last thing he wanted to do was steal away her smile by telling her about all his regrets.

Still, despite the lightness of the conversation and the sweet smiles from his daughters, Tanner's brain filled with a troubled darkness.

Why would Marceline have any reason to go into that barn? That particular one got very little traffic in the summer months, when the cattle and horses grazed on grass. Her presence there made absolutely no sense.

"Earth to Tanner." Josie's voice pierced through his thoughts. Her eyes were a beautiful golden green as she gazed at him. "What's wrong?"

"Nothing. Everything is fine."

She narrowed her eyes and shook a finger at him. "You can't fool me, Tanner Grange. You are definitely distracted and something is on your mind."

When had it happened that they'd gotten to know each other well enough to read each other's moods? He pushed his empty plate aside and raked a hand through his hair. "I saw Marceline earlier in a place she doesn't belong."

"What do you mean?"

"I saw her coming out of one of the barns and there's really no reason for her to be in there."

"Didn't you tell me she had a horse she visited regularly?"

"Yeah, but not in that barn," he replied.

"More, pease," Lily said and held up her plate.

Josie got up and gave the girls each a few more

chicken bites and then returned to the stool. "So, what are you thinking?"

He frowned. "I don't think you want to know what I'm thinking. I know you like her and she's been nice to you, but I'm hoping she doesn't have Eldridge tied up in that barn. Even worse, I'm hoping his dead body isn't there."

Josie gasped. "Do you really think that's possible? Wouldn't the sheriff and his people have already checked it out?"

He held her gaze for a long moment. "I'm sure they did on the day that Eldridge went missing, but I doubt that anyone has been in that barn since then. And yes, knowing Marceline, I think anything and everything is possible. I'm going to check it out when I go back outside."

"I want to go with you."

He looked at her in surprise. "There's no reason for you to go. Besides, I need you to stay here with the girls."

"I'll call Peggy. She'll look after them for a little while. Tanner, if Marceline has Eldridge in that barn, then I need to see it for myself." Her eyes glittered with a steely determination. "I need to know just how badly she's pulled the wool over my eyes. I need to know if the woman who I've invited in here is a murderer."

Despite his misgivings about having Josie come along, a half an hour later Peggy was watching the girls and he and Josie left the suite.

Josie walked close to him, bringing the scent of her into his head once again. Even though they hadn't talked about last night yet, he suspected before the day was over they were going to have to have a conversation about it.

But now wasn't the time or place. Right now all he could think about was that barn and what horrors they might possibly find inside. "I shouldn't have let you come with me."

She shot him one of her cheeky grins. "What makes you think you could stop me? Besides, I've been cooped up inside and it feels good to be outside in the sunshine for a few minutes."

As they continued to walk, her gaze swept the area, as did his. He knew she was looking for the man who they both knew had broken into her room, the same man who had confronted them by the tree with a gun in his hand.

This was the first time since arriving at the ranch that Josie had been outside and walking around. Was the man someplace nearby? Watching them right now?

He only saw two men as they walked and Tanner recognized both of them as part of the security team that had worked on the ranch for several years. Still, he was on full alert, his body tensed with a flood of fight-or-flight adrenaline against any danger that might appear.

The closer they moved toward the hay barn, the closer Josie walked against his side. "You know Marceline is one of few at the top of the suspect list," he said, breaking the silence between them.

"I know, but from everything I've heard, Fowler and Whitney have a lot more to gain than anyone else with Eldridge being dead," she replied. "I just can't believe Marceline had anything to do with her stepfather's disappearance. I don't want to believe it about her."

If Marceline did have something to do with it, then she had to be working with somebody. There was no way Marceline would have been able to subdue Eldridge and then force him out of the window all by herself.

She had no real friends or allies around the ranch, but she'd certainly managed to manipulate Josie's emotions. Who else might she have manipulated in order to get rid of Eldridge? And why had she refused to answer any of Troy's questions as to where she had been on the night Eldridge had disappeared?

What did she have to fear by talking to Troy? Tanner knew from the staff gossip that nobody had seen her around the house on the night Eldridge had disappeared. She'd come in early the next morning, so where had she been all night long and what had she been doing?

It wasn't uncommon for Marceline to go in and out of the barn where she stabled her horse. She might have many faults, but she did love her horse with a passion.

But her horse wasn't in this barn. This barn held

nothing but hay, and she sure as heck hadn't been in here to grab a bale of hay for her horse.

And she'd hated Eldridge with a passion.

"You don't think Marceline could have anything to do with the man who is after me, do you?" Josie asked.

He shot her a quick glance of surprise. "To be honest, it never entered my mind."

"I know it's a crazy idea, but if we're talking crazy then is it possible that she somehow met the man who is after the watch and he agreed to split whatever treasure we find with her? Maybe she's been making nice to me to see if I'll mention the watch and then they'll know for sure whether I have it in my possession or not."

"Sounds like a bit of a stretch," Tanner replied.

"To me, too," she replied with a touch of obvious relief in her voice.

Still, now that she'd put out the idea, he worked it around in his head. A bit of a stretch, yes...but also a faint possibility. Although it was hard to imagine Marceline lowering herself to have any dealings with the scraggly-haired, dirty gunman, he had no idea what lengths she might go to if she thought there was a pot of gold at the end of the deal.

And now that Josie had mentioned it, he couldn't get it out of his mind, and that only made him more nervous about what they might find in the barn.

When they reached the closed barn door where he'd seen Marceline sneak out, he drew his gun and his heart began to beat wildly. A sense of dread filled him as he turned to look at Josie.

"No matter what happens, stay behind me," he said and then he opened the door.

Chapter 10

He didn't have to tell her twice to stay behind him. As they entered the big barn Josie nearly stepped on his heels in an effort to stay close to him and his gun.

Her chest had tightened the moment they had left the house and her heart had begun to race with an unnatural pace. The taste of fear filled her mouth and she knew it wouldn't go away until they were back safely in the suite.

The idea that the woman she'd welcomed into the suite with Lily and Leigh might be capable of kidnapping or killing her stepfather filled Josie with a faint nausea. Had she misjudged the woman so badly?

Sunlight danced in through the high windows of

the barn, but there were plenty of areas in dark shadows, plenty of areas where a man could be held bound and gagged or a body could be hidden. There were also spaces where a gunman could hide and wait for the perfect opportunity.

The barn smelled of the hay bales that were stacked in tall columns. Surely if a dead body was in here they would smell decay. The thought churned her stomach. She didn't know much about human decomposition. Eldridge had been missing almost two weeks now. Maybe the smell of death would already be gone.

As she followed Tanner farther into the building, she shook her head in an attempt to rid herself of such horrible thoughts. But she couldn't help it when the memories of her mother's dead body on the ground and the man that Desmond had killed both jumped into her head.

Mommy, wake up!

Don't let Desmond see you!

Too much death. There had been too much violent death in her life.

She desperately hoped Marceline had nothing to do with Eldridge's disappearance, but admitted to herself that despite the short, friendly visits, she didn't know Marceline well. Had the pretty woman made an unholy alliance with a man seeking a buried treasure? Was money that important to her?

The silence in the barn felt heavy, pregnant with dire possibilities, and Josie found herself holding her breath in dreadful anticipation.

They moved methodically with Tanner checking every crease and crevice between the stacks of hay. Josie's heart thundered so loudly it beat in her ears with a discordant clang.

Would the mystery of Eldridge's disappearance be solved right now, right here in this barn? Was it possible the woman who had brought her friendship roses had also killed her own stepfather in cold blood?

She didn't know how much time passed when they'd circled the entire floor and found nobody there. Tanner finally holstered his gun, a deep frown creasing his brow. "Let's get the hell out of here."

They left the barn and headed back to the suite. Josie stayed close to his side and his hand never left the butt of his gun.

She wanted to be relieved that they'd found nothing in the barn, but that didn't explain why Marceline had been in there in the first place and there was still no answer as to what had happened to Eldridge Colton.

As much as she enjoyed Marceline's occasional visits, Josie now had serious questions about the woman's true character. One thing she had no question about was her feelings toward Tanner.

She was already eagerly anticipating the night to come. Hopefully she would share his bed again. Making love with him had been all kinds of wonderful, but awakening this morning with him spooned around her back and his arm around her waist had been nothing short of magical.

They entered the suite to find Peggy sitting in

the chair and Lily and Leigh playing on the floor in front of her. "Everything all right?" Peggy asked worriedly as she stood.

"As right as it can be for now," Tanner replied. "I just wish Troy would find Eldridge alive and things could go back to normal around here."

Peggy gave them a rueful smile. "*Normal* has never been a word I'd use around this ranch. I heard today that the blood on Mitchell Flunt's boots was his own and not Mr. Eldridge's. He's still being charged with theft, but he's been taken off the suspect list for having anything to do with Mr. Eldridge's disappearance."

"And that means Troy will be more focused than ever on the rest of the family," Tanner said.

Lily stood and walked to Josie and threw her arms around her knees. "Up!"

Josie picked her up and held her close. It was unsettling to have thoughts of kidnapping and murder in her head while the innocence of Lily and Leigh was present in the room.

"Josie-love," Lily said and snuggled her head into the crook of Josie's neck.

Josie looked at Tanner in stunned amazement. It was the first time either of the girls had said her name, and the utter sweetness of the moment stole away any bad thoughts she might have momentarily entertained.

Peggy laughed. "Josie, it looks like you're officially on the same level as Daddy-love."

"Daddy-love," Leigh repeated and raced for Tanner's arms.

Tanner picked her up and then smiled at the older woman. "Thanks, Peggy, for helping us out. I can't tell you how much you're appreciated."

"No problem. You know I'm always available for you and the girls at any time of the day or night." With a murmured goodbye Peggy left.

"I'm going to head back outside until dinnertime," Tanner said and placed Leigh on the floor.

Josie frowned at him. "I wish you had that ranch of yours that you dream about so you could take these girls away from this place where you don't know who to trust," she said. "It's unsettling to think there might be a murderer here in the house."

Tanner held her gaze for a long moment. "That would be nice," he replied. "Someday I'll have that ranch and be my own boss and raise my girls in a real home. I'll see you later this afternoon." He turned and left.

Within ten minutes it was obvious the girls were ready for their afternoon nap. Once they were down, Josie sat in the chair by the window and stared outside, but her thoughts were far away from the landscape.

The last thing she wanted to think about was who was responsible for Eldridge's disappearance. Instead she closed her eyes and imagined being on a different ranch. It would be smaller than this one, with a rambling farmhouse and plenty of room to grow a family—her family with Tanner.

There would be a large kitchen where she'd make blueberry pancakes in the mornings and hardy dinners that would be warm and ready when Tanner knocked off work for the day.

Maybe, just maybe, after a year or so she could give him a son to carry on the Grange name. Lily and Leigh would make great big sisters to any siblings that were added to the family.

She wanted the fantasy to come true. She wanted to spend the rest of her life loving Tanner and Lily and Leigh. She couldn't help but believe he was in love with her, too.

Last night they hadn't just had sex. They had made wonderful, passionate love. She needed to get the watch into her father's hands and then come back here to start a real life together with Tanner.

She was ready for her future now and she wanted Tanner to know just how deeply she loved him. With plenty of time on her hands, she dug her cell phone out of her purse for a check-in call with Trevor.

He answered on the second ring. "I was just thinking about giving you a call," he said.

"Things have been pretty crazy around here."

"I've been following the case in the news reports," he replied. "Sounds like there haven't been many answers forthcoming."

"There haven't been, but the craziness hasn't just been about Eldridge." She told him about the break-in the night before. Trevor expressed his outrage and his ongoing concern with her safety.

"Tanner has my back," she replied. "He's been absolutely wonderful. Now, did you have a specific reason for thinking about calling me?"

"Yeah, although I hesitate to tell you now because I don't want you to put yourself at risk."

"Tell me anyway. I'm a big girl."

"Matthew isn't expected to live through the week. Josie, forget the watch. None of us want to see you in any more danger."

Josie frowned thoughtfully. "We promised him we'd get him the watch after he told us where Mother's body was buried."

"He ran us around for months with stupid clues when he could have just told us where she was," Trevor replied with a touch of disgust in his deep voice.

"I know, but I made a promise to him. I'll talk to Tanner and see if we can somehow sneak out in the next couple of nights and get the watch. Hopefully I can get it back in time."

"Just be careful, Josie girl. You're more important than any watch or promise we made to him."

Josie smiled into the phone. "Thanks, Trevor. I'll be in touch."

They ended the call. Trevor's concern washed over her in a wave of warmth. Being reunited with her brothers and sister had been a dream come true, although she still needed more time to get to know them all better. They had years to catch up on.

She'd grown particularly close to Trevor. Maybe it was because she had several vague memories of her oldest brother. She'd been only three when they'd all been placed in foster homes, but she remembered Trevor picking her up in his arms. "Josie girl," he'd called her then and he still called her that.

The next half hour flew by with her thinking about her siblings. Then the girls got up from their naps and the rest of the afternoon passed swiftly as they played together and waited for Daddy-love to come home.

Daddy-love.

Tanner, her love, her future. At least she hoped he was her future. She refused to allow any doubts to creep into her heart.

By the time Tanner returned to the suite, she had the girls in their stroller and ready to go to dinner. As they ate with the other staff members, Josie counted the minutes until they could once again be alone and she could tell him what was in her heart, confess to him the depth of her love.

It wasn't until after dinner and playtime was over and the girls were in their cribs for the night that she and Tanner were finally alone in the living room.

"Long day," she said as she accepted the glass of wine he'd poured for her. This was their evening ritual, a wind-down time after the girls were peacefully asleep that Josie relished.

He sat in the chair and released a deep sigh. "Crazy long," he agreed. "I have to admit, I was sure we'd find Eldridge in the barn."

"Thank goodness we didn't," she replied.

"I don't think he'll be found alive." His voice held an edge of grief.

She didn't try to fill him with false hope. After all the time that had passed, she believed more likely than not that Eldridge was dead, too. "I'm so sorry, Tanner. I know you cared about him."

He gave a curt nod. "I did... I do."

"Did you have a good relationship with your father?" she asked curiously. During all the conversations they'd shared, he hadn't said much about the parents he'd lost.

His features lightened. "I did. My father was my best friend and my mom was the greatest. I almost feel guilty saying that knowing your circumstances."

"Don't be silly," she replied. "This has nothing to do with me. Tell me more about them."

He took a drink of his beer and then continued, "Dad was the salt of the earth. He had a small spread not too far away from here and he loved my mother and me and that land. Unfortunately, when they died they were deeply in debt and so the ranch was sold to pay debts."

"But you followed in your father's footsteps."

He smiled, his eyes filled with the softness of memories. "I did. Dad tried to talk me into a dozen different occupations, but I think he was secretly thrilled when I told him all I wanted in life was to be a rancher like him." His smile slowly faded. "I know about your father, but do you have any memories of your mother? What was she like?"

Josie relaxed into the back of the chair. "I remember soft, loving hands, a beautiful smile and musical laughter. But almost all of what I know about her I've learned through my brothers and sister. They know more about her than me because I was so young when she was murdered."

"Was she a full-time mother?"

"With seven children she had to be, but she also worked at home as a seamstress. I'm sure they needed any of the money she made because the ranch where we lived wasn't a working ranch and my father only did odd jobs as a handyman."

"I'm so glad you have your brothers and sister now," he said.

"Me, too, and I'm glad you had Eldridge to help you through what must have been some dark days," she replied.

"There definitely were some dark days," he agreed. "I just hope we get some sort of closure soon where Eldridge is concerned. I hope whoever is guilty is caught and punished."

"I'm sure Troy and his team will accomplish that. He seems like a good man."

"He is," he agreed. He offered her a small smile. "He was smart enough to clear you."

"Thank goodness. He's definitely got enough suspects without me on the list." She finished the last of her wine and set the glass on a coaster on the end table.

He took a drink from his beer and then cleared his throat. "Josie, if you don't feel safe sleeping in your own room tonight then you can have my bed and I'll bunk out here on the sofa."

She stared at him in shock, but he didn't meet her gaze. Instead he looked down at the floor just in front of his chair. "Why would you do that?" she asked.

He took another drink of his beer before finally looking at her. "Josie, last night shouldn't have happened and the last thing I want is for us to make another mistake."

She leaned forward and held his gaze intently. "Last night wasn't a mistake, Tanner. I told you no regrets and I meant it. What we shared was beautiful."

"It was, but it won't happen again." His features were closed off, his eyes shuttered and impossible to read.

She swallowed against the words of love that had trembled on her lips all evening. Now wasn't the time to tell him how she felt about him. He was obviously feeling guilty or something about the night before, even though he had no reason to feel that way.

"I'll be fine in my own room tonight."

The relief that washed over his face was like a tentative stab through her heart. Still, it wasn't a killing wound and she told herself that sooner or later the right time would come for her to let him know that she was in love with him.

"So, we're good?" he asked.

"We're good," she replied. She just had to show him that she was the woman to fill his life with joy and love. She just had to give him time to realize they belonged together forever.

Troy Watkins looked up from his desk as his right-hand man, Charlie Kidwell, walked into his office. "Hey, boss, you wanted an update?" The tall, blond deputy threw himself into the straight-back chair in front of the desk.

"Tell me something good," Troy said.

The thirty-five-year-old man frowned, his blue eyes radiating the same weariness that tugged at Troy's very bones. "Wish I had something good to report. We've investigated the alibis of most of the Colton ranch hands and they all check out. We're still trying to substantiate alibis for some of the house staff and the family. You know it all takes time."

"I know. I'm just so frustrated. I was hoping the blood on Flunt's work boots would belong to Eldridge and we could get this case solved once and for all," Troy replied.

"We need a body. There's so little forensic evidence and if we could find his body then maybe we'd get lucky by finding some real, substantial evidence."

Troy reared back in his chair. "Eldridge was a sly one, telling Hugh Barrington the will can't be opened without his body."

"How does that work legally?" Charlie asked.

"Hell if I know. That's something for Hugh and the family to work out within the mishmash of legalese." He frowned thoughtfully. "I can't help but think that whoever did this was close to Eldridge."

"You mean like a family member."

Troy shrugged. "Or a member of the staff. Somehow the perp had to know Eldridge was in his bedroom all alone that night. They had to have known he was vulnerable at that particular time."

"And that points the finger to Whitney."

"Or somebody who saw her asleep in the media room and knew Eldridge was ripe for the picking." Troy leaned forward and slapped his palms down on the top of the desk. "Damn, but this case is eating me alive. Get back out there and get me something."

Charlie stood. "We're doing everything we can. Hopefully something will happen to break the case."

Troy nodded wearily and released a deep sigh as Charlie left the room.

He had members of the Colton family chewing his butt for answers, the press clamoring every day for more information and he'd never felt so impotent in his entire life.

They had searched nearly every inch of the Colton Valley Ranch and no body had turned up. He'd watched all the tapes from the security cameras around the place and they had yielded nothing, either.

The men and women working for him were functioning on overtime hours and already half of them were burned out by this case. He knew he had to widen the search area. He was going to have to make arrangements to drain the nearby Lone Star Lake, a lake deep enough for a body to be weighed down and hidden in the dark depths.

And his brain thundered day and night with the question of just where in the hell was Eldridge Colton?

Saturday morning Josie awoke with a new optimism. Today she was making chicken and dumplings and chocolate chip cookies, and hopefully Tanner would come to his senses after last night's bout of guilt over something he shouldn't feel guilty about at all. They were both consenting adults. He hadn't taken advantage of her in any way.

He was quiet as they worked together to get the girls their breakfast. "Looks like it's going to be another stifling day," she said as she cleaned up a handful of strawberries.

"Mid-July in Texas is always stifling hot," he replied. He stared at the toaster as if it were the most fascinating appliance he'd ever seen.

"It will be so beautiful in the fall," she said, remembering the lighthearted argument they'd had about seasons.

He merely nodded as the toast popped up. Josie swallowed a sigh and placed the strawberries on the girls' plates. Drat the man anyway.

"Josie-love." Leigh held out a strawberry toward her.

Josie smiled. "You eat it."

Leigh popped it into her mouth and then grinned at Josie.

Love pooled in the center of Josie's heart. "Josie loves Leigh and Lily," she said.

Tanner placed toast on the girls' plates. "I'd better get to work."

"Have a nice day and we'll see you later," Josie replied.

He kissed each of the twins and then left the suite.

He'd barely looked at her and he certainly hadn't indulged in any small talk. Frustration gnawed at Josie as she cleaned up the breakfast dishes.

She'd halfway hoped that by this morning he would have come to his senses and let go of whatever silly guilt he felt about what they had shared.

Still, the day stretched out with promise, and maybe tonight with their chicken and dumplings he'd change his mind and she could tell him what was really in her heart for him.

After lunch when the twins went down for their naps, Josie got to work in the kitchen.

The liberated women of today would probably laugh at her for finding so much pleasure in cooking for a man, she thought as she peeled carrots and cut up celery to add to the cooking chicken and broth.

She wanted to comfort Tanner with good food, with warm body heat and with enduring love. She refused to be too concerned by his attitude last night and this morning. She was willing to be patient with him, to allow him to come to the realization that they belonged together.

She was almost pleased when there was no visit from Marceline. After the barn hunt yesterday and Tanner's concern that the young woman might be involved with Eldridge's disappearance, it would have been difficult for her to sit and share idle chitchat with her today.

Tanner had wondered why on earth Marceline was being so sociable to Josie. Now that she'd considered the remote possibility Marceline might be in cahoots with the man in the woods, she was definitely more than a bit wary of the pretty young woman.

She shoved these troubling thoughts out of her head. All she wanted to think about now was Tanner and the girls and fixing them a meal served with love.

By the time the twins got up from their naps, the suite smelled of fragrant chicken and vegetables and she was ready to make the dumplings and stir up the batter for the chocolate chip cookies.

As she worked the two girls played at her feet, banging together a variety of pots and pans and measuring cups. Their noisy play only added to the music that sang in Josie's soul.

She could have this every day—children playing at her feet, good food cooking on the stove and a man who lit up her heart as nobody else might ever do.

When Tanner walked through the door at four

thirty, she had the girls in their high chairs, the island set for two and a smile of welcome on her lips.

"Something smells delicious," he said after he'd kissed his girls hello.

"And it's ready to eat whenever you are."

"I'll just get out of my work clothes and I'll be ready." He disappeared into the bedroom and Josie released a sigh of frustration. He'd scarcely looked at her. Why was he being so silly? He had no reason to suffer from any guilt over making love to her.

When he returned to the living room a few minutes later, Josie put on her happy face, determined to turn things around between them.

"Did you have a good day?" she asked as she dished up the meal.

"The usual." He eased down on one of the stools at the island. "Were the girls good for you today?"

"They're always good. Well, Lily did attempt to color on the wall in the nursery and Leigh had a bit of a temper tantrum when I put the colors away, but stuff like that isn't extraordinary for life with eighteen-month-old twins, right?"

"Right."

"As soon as we finish eating, I've got the cookies ready to go into the oven. I want you to taste them while they're nice and warm."

"Sounds good," he agreed.

The meal was excruciating as she tried to engage him and he remained distant. He answered her questions in as few words as possible and kept his gaze focused on everything in the room except her.

By the time she pulled the chocolate chip cookies out of the oven, she wanted to scream at him, but she didn't. She swallowed her frustration and forged ahead with a smile.

"If you tell me these are no better than your boxed cookies I'll have to strangle you," she said teasingly as she placed two cookies on a small platter before him.

"Mmm," Lily said as she bit into a cookie.

"Mmm, good," Leigh exclaimed.

Tanner offered a small smile. "They're definitely a hit with the younger crowd."

Josie drank in the beauty of his smile. She sat next to him at the island and gestured toward his platter. "And now I want to hear, what do you think?"

He bit into a cookie. "Mmm, good," he said with a light sparkle in his eyes. "Definitely better than store-bought."

"I rest my case," she replied, grateful that the cookies seemed to have broken through his moody silence. "Want another one?"

"Please," he replied.

"More," Lily said. "More cookie, pease." Leigh echoed the sentiment and Josie's heart warmed with pleasure.

A few minutes later she cleaned up the kitchen while Tanner played with the girls in the nursery. The cookies had broken the ice between them for only a hot minute. As soon as he'd eaten the last crumb, he'd again grown quiet and distant. Once again she told herself what he needed was time to process how quickly their relationship had ignited and deepened.

Just because she knew how she felt about him didn't mean he was in the same place yet. She could be patient. *Good things come to those who wait*, she reminded herself.

Immediately after they put the twins to bed, Tanner called it a night and disappeared into his bedroom. She sat in the living room for a while by herself.

She wondered if he'd really take to the sofa if she appeared in his bedroom doorway like she had before. Would he give in to temptation once again or would he grab a blanket and his gun and reject her?

After the night they had just had, she knew he'd move to the sofa. Time, she once again reminded herself. She was expecting too much too soon from him.

But over the next three days Tanner remained distant and aloof. Their routine remained the same with one exception. Each evening when the girls were put to bed, he immediately retired to his bedroom.

However, in the time they were together sharing a meal or playing with the twins, Josie swore she felt a yearning from him. At times his eyes were soft and warm on her and at other times they held a hint of heated hunger.

On this particular evening, her frustration with him had grown to a fever pitch. Together they put the girls to bed for the night and then he murmured a good-night to her and disappeared into his bedroom.

Josie sat on the sofa and steamed. It was as if he were punishing her because he'd wanted her, because she'd wanted him. It wasn't fair and it wasn't right.

She stood, deciding it was past time she confronted him about how he'd been acting toward her for the past seven days. His bedroom door was partially closed, but she threw it fully open as if she had the right.

Chapter 11

He was still dressed and stretched out on his bed with his pillows plumped behind him and a magazine open in his lap. As she entered, he looked up, obviously startled.

"Josie, is something wrong?" he asked with a touch of alarm.

"As a matter of fact, something is." She leaned against the door and narrowed her eyes. "It's wrong that you have been treating me like a pariah ever since the night we made love. It's definitely wrong that you refuse to look me in the eyes, that you barely talk to me and that you run in here and hide from me the minute the girls go to sleep each night."

He sat up, a dusty red creeping into his cheeks.

"I haven't been hiding out. I've just been unusually tired over the last few days."

She narrowed her eyes at what she knew was a blatant lie. "Really? Tired?" She shook her head. "That's bull and you know it, Tanner. I think you're not only beating yourself up for making love with me, but you're also punishing me."

"I'm not punishing anyone," he protested, but he didn't quite meet her gaze.

"What are you afraid of, Tanner?"

His gaze connected with hers once again. "I'm not afraid of anything," he protested with a raise of his chin.

"You want to know what I believe? I think you're afraid of loving me." Her words hung in the air for several long moments and when he didn't immediately speak she finally continued.

"I'm in love with you, Tanner. I want to spend the rest of my life with you and Lily and Leigh. I want to lie in your arms at night and laugh with you during the days."

He stared at her and got off the bed. No joy leaped into his darkened eyes. No sudden epiphany curved his lips into an exuberant smile. Instead he looked at her as if she'd lost her ever-loving mind.

"Josie, you don't know what you're saying. This, us… It's just not right. Whatever you think you feel for me, it isn't real. We've just been through some traumatic events."

"Don't tell me what's real and what isn't." She took

a step toward him and was vaguely surprised when he took a step back as if not wanting her anywhere near him. "My feelings for you have nothing to do with things that have happened here outside of you and me. Tanner, I know what's in my heart. I love you and I want to spend the rest of my life with you."

"I have nothing to give you," he replied and shoved his hands into his pockets. "I have no intention of ever marrying again. I'm not even in the market for a long-term relationship."

She searched his stoic features. He looked so handsome in his jeans and the blue T-shirt that enhanced the color of his eyes. But it wasn't just his physical appearance that pulled such a wealth of love for him into her heart, and there was no way she believed he was as blasé about her, about them, as he pretended in this moment.

She frowned as a new thought entered her mind. "Is it because you're still in love with Helen?" she asked. "Because if that's true, then it's a real tragedy. Helen is gone and she's never coming back. If you don't let her go to allow new love into your life then that means Lily and Leigh will never have the love of a mother figure in their lives."

His eyebrows rose and then fell into a frown. "I can be enough for my girls. Besides, I'm not still in love with my ex-wife."

"But you told me you still loved her when she left you." Josie wanted to understand—what was happening? What was really keeping him from her?

"That lasted until I realized Helen wasn't coming back to see the girls, that she had no intention of them having anything to do with her new life. My love for her died a cold, hard death before she was ever killed in the car accident."

A sliver of relief rushed through Josie. She knew she could never compete with a ghost and she believed his words. She took another step toward him, her heart nearly beating out of her chest. "Then why are you so afraid of loving me?"

"You're too young for me, Josie, and that's something you can't fix and you can't change. We should have never kissed. We definitely shouldn't have made love because as I said before, I have nothing to give to you."

His cold tone and flat, emotionless eyes sliced a knife through her heart. She stared at him for several long, charged moments.

"You're a fool, Tanner Grange," she finally said. She whirled around and left the room before he could see the tears that burned at her eyes.

She escaped into the nursery, where she sat in a chair at the little table where she'd colored with the twins, where they'd played with toys and they'd fed her pretend "'sgetti" and cookies and juice.

Tears seeped down her cheeks as she breathed in the sweet scent of baby lotion and heard the little puffy breaths that Lily always made when she slept and thought about the soft little blanket that Leigh always pressed against her heart when she slept.

This was where she belonged. She felt it in her heart, in her soul. She also believed Tanner loved her, but she didn't know what to do to make him embrace his feelings for her.

Too young.

It would have been laughable if it wasn't so absolutely heartbreaking. He was only looking at a number rather than looking at her.

She wasn't too young. She'd lived a lifetime of heartaches and had more life experience than people three times her age. She knew with certainty what she wanted and she was more than ready to be his wife and a mother to his children.

But it didn't matter what she wanted. Her love for him meant nothing if he wouldn't accept it. A sob choked out of her and she quickly stood and ran into her bedroom before the sound of her cries could awaken the twins.

She threw herself facedown on the yellow bedspread and muffled her cries with a pillow. The pain of broken dreams, of beautiful fantasies that would never come true, stabbed through her.

He was right. She couldn't change it and she couldn't fix it. She couldn't magically change her age or his mind. She'd told him how much she loved him. She'd told him that she wanted to spend the rest of her life with him, and he'd rejected her.

She'd truly believed if she told him how she felt about him he would respond by telling her he loved her, that he wanted her in his life forever. But that hadn't happened and it wasn't going to happen.

It was time to leave.

She cried until there were no tears left inside her. She remained on her bed, hoping—praying—Tanner would come to her, take her into his arms and tell her that he had been a fool and that he loved her and wanted her as his wife, as his partner.

But minutes ticked by…then an hour and then another hour and that didn't happen. The suite was quiet and in darkness except for the night-light that cast illumination in the nursery and the bright moonlight that danced through her bedroom window.

The thought of getting up in the morning and pretending her world was right was nauseating. The idea of spending more time with Tanner and the girls knowing she would never, ever be a permanent member of the family was torturous.

She would now be an outsider here, as she'd been for most of her life. With every minute that passed she would be reminded that she had no place here except as a temporary nanny.

Yes, it was definitely time to leave.

Peggy would probably be glad to step in and help Tanner with the girls until he could find a new nanny, and it was better to leave now before the twins got too attached to her.

Josie-love. Her heart squeezed tight and the back of her throat threatened to close up with new tears. Over the past week both Lily and Leigh had called her that. She only wished their father would call her that, too. She only wished…

It was just after midnight when she crept out of her bedroom and down the hallway. Her suitcase weighed heavily in her hand. It was filled not only with the items she'd brought with her to the ranch, but also the burden of unrequited love.

When she passed Tanner's bedroom, the weight got heavier and new tears burned hot, tears she quickly swallowed against. She wouldn't shed another tear over him.

It was over. It was done, and it was time for her to remember why she'd come here in the first place, the mission her family had tasked her with.

Trevor had told her that Matthew might not last the week. It was time to get the job done and return to Granite Gulch. Her father would have his precious watch and life would go on.

She paused in the kitchen and opened a drawer and removed a small paring knife. Carefully she stuck it into her pocket. Hopefully the only thing she'd need to use it on was the hard Texas soil when she dug for the watch.

Thankfully she managed to get out of the suite without Tanner awakening. The last thing she wanted was another confrontation with him.

She stood in the dark hallway just outside of the door for a long moment, her heart saying the good-byes she wouldn't be here to say in person.

She imagined the sweet skin of Leigh's cheek as

she kissed her and the way Lily liked to wind her fingers into Josie's hair. The sound of their giggles when Josie tickled them filled her head with a grief that made her want to fall to her knees.

She allowed the piercing grief to suffuse her for only a moment, and then with a determined grip of the suitcase handle, she headed down the hallway to exit the building.

She slid outside the door, where the moonlight made it easy for her to load her suitcase and purse into her car. With her belongings stowed away, she paused by the side of the driver door and looked around.

Hopefully she'd managed to get out of the building without anyone seeing her. This was probably better than her and Tanner trying to sneak out in the middle of the night. Two people would be more easily spotted than one.

She started walking across the lawn toward the tree in the woods, where hopefully she could dig up the watch. The only things she carried with her were her cell phone and the knife she'd taken to help her dig in the hard dirt.

Hurrying across the land, she knew she had a fairly long walk to reach the tree. Her senses were all on high alert. She was aware the moonlight that aided her along the way might also make her a visible target.

She attempted to use the shadow of trees to hide her presence. The last thing she wanted was for the gunman to see her, but she also didn't want to run into any of the security team and have to explain what she was doing outside in the middle of the night.

All she wanted was to get the darned watch for her father and escape this place of heartbreak. She thought of Trevor's words that their father was fading fast and the doctors weren't giving him much more time.

Even if she hadn't left the house tonight, she would have asked Tanner to take her back to the tree in the next day or two. Now she wouldn't have to ask the man she loved for anything. She'd take care of it herself and then be gone.

Her feelings where her father was concerned were certainly a jumbled mess. She hated him for what he was, for what he had done to wreak havoc on so many lives, but there was still a little girl inside of her who desperately wanted to love the man who was her father.

She could have just gotten into her car and driven away. Still, even with everything that had happened, she didn't want to leave here without the watch. She didn't care whether it was a clue to hidden treasures or merely a piece of junk her father wanted. She just wanted to do what she'd told her siblings she'd do. She wanted to get one thing right.

Finally she reached the wooded area where Tanner had parked his truck when they'd come here before. It was much darker here with the moonlight barely filtering through the thick tree leaves.

Once again she paused before continuing forward. Her heart thrummed a frantic rhythm and she prayed that nobody had followed her here. She didn't sense anyone close by, but she wasn't sure she could trust her own instincts anymore. She'd sensed Tanner had loved her and that had certainly proved false.

She pulled her cell phone from her pocket and turned on the function that was a tiny beam of light. A shiver waltzed up her spine as she took a step forward and then paused again to look left, then right and then behind her.

A rustling noise froze her in her tracks. Her heart crashed against her ribs with a frenzied pounding. Her breath caught in the back of her throat, making it difficult to draw a breath.

Was it him? Was he here? Had he been watching and waiting? Had he seen her leave the house and followed her and was now ready to pounce?

The rustling noise sounded closer…near her feet. She pointed her beam down and in the bottom of a thick bush she spied two bandit eyes staring at her.

A raccoon. Thank God it was nothing bigger and meaner. Thank God it wasn't a man with a gun. The animal scurried away and her breath shuddered out of her on a sigh of relief. She could deal with night creatures of the animal kind. What she didn't want to encounter was a creature of the human kind.

She hurried forward, careful to make as little noise as possible and keeping her light focused on the ground so she didn't trip. She didn't want a fall that could break an arm or a leg.

The sound of the stream on her left side assured

her that she was headed in the right direction. *Get the watch and go home. Get the watch and go home.* The words played over and over again in her head.

Finally she reached the tree. She fell to her knees at the base, just beneath the mysterious carvings that had been slashed into the trunk years ago.

She pulled the knife out of her pocket and slashed it into the ground. The dry earth was hard, but the knife worked some magic and broke it apart. When she'd broken up the dirt enough, she began to scoop it with her hands, seeking the long-buried watch that her father had said would be here.

She didn't know how long she dug, using the knife and then her hands over and over again without finding anything. Momentarily exhausted by her exertions, she sat back on her haunches and frowned.

Was this just another one of her father's manipulations? Was there even a watch buried here? He'd certainly enjoyed giving his children vague clues over a long period of time when they'd been trying to find where he'd buried their mother's body.

It had only been when he'd given them the final clue of "blue" that Josie had remembered that sky-colored splash of paint on the old fence by the barn on the family homestead and they'd realized it was where he'd placed their mother.

At first all of them had thought about having her body moved to a cemetery, but in the end they had made the decision to leave her where she was, undisturbed in her final resting place. They had all gone to that place on the old homestead and she'd been mourned by all her children who had grown up without her loving presence.

Would Matthew send her here on a wild-goose chase for a watch that didn't even exist? She chewed her bottom lip thoughtfully. But the gunman had said Matthew had bragged about the watch, that he'd told others about it.

Obviously the man who had been more than a thorn in their sides believed the watch not only existed, but also held a clue to a stash of money.

She bent forward and began to dig again in frustration, now not knowing if this was just one of her father's sick games or if she would really find his old watch.

She widened the hole, wincing as she broke a nail in her frantic efforts. She dug faster, aware that every minute she was here was a minute when danger could come out of nowhere.

Tink.

Her fingernails glanced off something that felt like metal. Her heart began to race again as she scrabbled to move the dirt away enough that she could grab the item.

Success. She pulled the round item from the dirt and then grabbed her cell phone light to look at it. A roar of excitement shot through her. A pocket watch with a piece of chain still connected to the fob. The chain was rusty, as was the watch itself, but the dirty old pocket watch felt wonderful in her grasp.

She quickly moved the dirt back into the hole and then got to her feet and shoved the watch and the knife into her pocket. Now all she needed to do was get back to her car and head to Granite Gulch. She would see to it that her father had the watch before he died. Mission accomplished.

"Josie Colton, we meet again."

She froze in horror. The deep voice came out of the darkness to her left and her heart crashed to the pit of her stomach as the same man stepped into view with his gun pointed at her chest.

Tanner awoke with a start. He sat up and listened, but heard nothing but silence in the suite. He lay back down and looked at the clock on his nightstand. Just after midnight. He'd been asleep for only about a half an hour.

The second most difficult thing he had done in his life had been to keep himself isolated and distant from Josie for the past several days. The first most difficult thing he'd done was listen to her pour her heart out to him and virtually turn his back on her.

She had looked so beautiful when she'd burst into his room. Her cheeks had been flushed with a hot pink that matched her blouse and her eyes had sparked like a warrior woman on a quest.

Having to completely turn off his emotions from her had broken more than a piece of his heart even as he'd known he was breaking her.

However, he knew rejecting her was for the best,

not just for her but for him and his daughters as well. The last thing he wanted was another broken relationship. The last thing he wanted for his daughters was for them to get closer to Josie, to love her even more than they did and have her walk away when they were old enough to feel her absence.

And eventually she would have walked away from him…from them. He was absolutely certain of that fact. She hadn't experienced enough of real life to know if she was truly ready to be a wife, to be a mother.

He suspected she'd been hiding out here not only from an armed man who wanted her father's old watch, but also from getting on with the rest of her life.

She'd had only a month of freedom after years of being in the witness protection program. Decisions had been made for her all of her life, first in foster care and then in protective custody. It had to be daunting to finally be free to make choices for herself and to try to figure out exactly what she wanted her life to be.

Believing she was in love with him was too easy. She might be happy here for a couple of months, but eventually she would have realized she'd jumped too fast and she would want to explore being young and beautiful and completely unencumbered.

He'd watched helplessly as Helen had turned her back on him and the twins. He didn't want to see another woman walk away from them. He wasn't going to give another woman the opportunity, especially one he knew was just too young to know what she really wanted.

Still, the pain he'd caused had radiated from her beautiful eyes and cut him to his core. He cared about her deeply. He cared enough about her to push her away, to force her to find the life she deserved.

Unable to go back to sleep, he got up and pulled on his jeans and a T-shirt and then grabbed his gun and padded into the living room. He sank down on the sofa and wondered what the morning might bring.

Troy had said Josie could leave whenever she wanted. She was free to go home to Granite Gulch. She owed him and his girls nothing and he knew tonight he'd broken her heart completely.

Would she pack up and leave when she woke up? Would she stay to see to it that the girls had their breakfast and then leave?

An ache filled his chest as he thought about her not being in his life anymore. She'd take so much of the warmth in his heart with her. She'd steal away so much of the laughter when she left. She would definitely take a huge piece of his heart with her, but he couldn't tell her that. The last thing he wanted was to give her any false hope that there could ever be something between them.

Restless energy filled him and he got up off the sofa and paced the length of the living room several times. He didn't even remember his heart being this heavy when Helen had walked out of their marriage.

Knowing he needed to get some sleep before morning, he got off the sofa and walked down the hall. But instead of turning into his own room, he continued on down the hall. The need to take a peek at his sleeping daughters drove him into the nursery.

As usual, Leigh slept on her tummy, her head turned to the side and her favorite blanket clutched in one hand. Lily slept on her back, sprawled as if she owned the bed and all the space around her.

They loved Josie and he didn't question that Josie loved them. She would have made a wonderful mother to them, if only she were even five years older…ten years older.

The ache in his heart only expanded. Josie was right. If he kept himself closed off from the possibility of ever finding love again then his daughters would never know the love of a mother in their lives.

But he couldn't make his romantic decisions based on his daughters. And he couldn't love Josie Colton. He refused to love her. He turned away from the cribs and stared at the partially opened doorway that led into Josie's room.

The light was out and no sound came from within. He'd heard her weeping after she'd run from his room. Each one of her sobs, every one of her tears, had ripped at his heart.

He stared at the doorway, and just as he'd needed to get a glance of his daughters, he wanted to look at Josie while she slept. For all he knew, he might never get the opportunity again to gaze at her while she was vulnerable.

He crept to the doorway and peered inside. The bright moonlight gave him a perfect view of the bed…the very empty bed. His brain worked to make sense of the fact that she wasn't in the room. She hadn't been in the guest bathroom when he'd passed by it.

She was gone.

A wild panic hurtled through him. Had she sneaked out of the suite and to her car and driven away? Or had she gone after that damn watch all alone in the middle of the night?

He walked over to a drawer where he knew she'd kept her things and pulled it open. Empty. She had definitely packed up her things, but had she left the property?

He hurried back to his room, where he turned on the bedside light, grabbed his keys from the nightstand and then raced for the front door. Under most circumstances he would never, ever leave his girls alone for a single minute, but this wasn't most circumstances.

Besides, it would take him only a couple of minutes at the most to see if Josie's car was still parked outside. He hurried down the hallway toward the door that led outside, his heart beginning an unnatural racing rhythm.

He opened the door and his worst thoughts were realized. Her car was still there, but she was nowhere in sight. He turned and hurried back down the hallway.

Once inside the suite he didn't hesitate to grab his phone and call Peggy. Despite the lateness of the hour, she answered on the second ring, sounding alert and wide-awake.

"Peggy, I need you." His voice cracked with emotion he hadn't yet processed. "I think Josie is in trouble."

"I'll be right there."

Tanner hung up and grabbed his holster. He slung it on around his waist and shoved his gun into it. His heart now thundered with barely suppressed fear.

Why hadn't she asked him to go with her to get the watch? Why would she take off all alone in the dark of night? The answers were easy. It was because she didn't trust him anymore. It was because he'd broken her heart.

Damn her for putting herself at risk to make a dying serial killer happy. He could only hope the gunman wasn't on the property and hadn't seen her take off on her own.

He grabbed a flashlight from beneath the kitchen sink counter and then stood in the middle of the living room with every muscle tensed as he waited for Peggy to arrive. When had Josie left the suite? Had it been the sound of her going out the door that had awakened him?

How long ago had that been? Twenty minutes? Thirty?

He was half-frantic by the time Peggy arrived. "I don't know how long I'll be gone. Feel free to sleep on the sofa until I get back. I just couldn't leave the girls here all alone."

"Of course you couldn't. Go," she exclaimed. "Go do whatever it is you need to do and don't worry about things here. Just make sure Josie is safe."

Tanner nodded and then hurried out the door. Yes, he definitely wanted to keep Josie safe. When he reached the outside, he headed for the stable where he kept Beau. Josie was on foot and hopefully he could catch up with her if he was on horseback. He wanted to get to her before she got to that cursed tree.

He'd like to take one of the trucks, but at this time of night he feared he'd awaken everyone in the big house and he wouldn't put it past Fowler to fire him. Besides, the horse would be almost as fast.

He saddled Beau in record time and then mounted and took off across the pasture. In spite of Zane's added security, he saw nobody as he rode hell-bent for leather toward the wooded area in the distance.

Even without an armed man hunting for her, Josie could encounter all kinds of troubles in the dark in the woods. She was unfamiliar with the area. She could fall and break a leg or slip and knock herself unconscious.

Or the creep who had been shadowing her could find her again…find her out here alone and vulnerable. His fear for her exploded through his veins. His one driving thought was to get to her as quickly as possible. His single driving need at the moment was to make sure she was okay.

Once again he wondered when she had left the suite. How long of a head start did she have on him?

With every second he didn't see her, his heart beat faster.

The heat of the night nearly suffocated him. Or was it his fear for her that closed up the back of his throat and made his chest heavy and breathing difficult?

It seemed to take forever to ride across the pasture even though he knew it had taken him only a few minutes. When he reached the edge of the woods, he got off Beau and tied the reins to a low tree branch. Then he set off on foot with the flashlight beam leading the way.

He'd hoped to catch up to her before now. Was she already at the tree? If she was, then hopefully she was there all alone and he'd run into her as she was heading back to the ranch.

He moved as quickly as possible through the trees and shrub. He didn't bother to call her name. He didn't trust she would answer him. If she'd wanted him with her she wouldn't have left all alone; she would have asked him to accompany her.

At least the woods weren't filled with her screams. His stomach clenched at the very thought of her ever having a reason to scream.

He was within twenty yards of the tree when the sound of voices broke the silence. All of his muscles tensed and he quickly turned off the flashlight.

"I didn't find anything." Josie's strained voice rose in volume. "It was supposed to be here, but it wasn't."

"Don't lie to me, girl."

Tanner instantly recognized the deep snarl. He pulled his gun and crept closer, needing to get a visual on the situation. He slid behind a tree trunk and peeked around it.

His heart felt like it stopped. Josie stood on his left and the man stood to his right with his gun leveled at Josie's chest. Danger crackled in the air like the precursor of a lightning strike.

"I'm not lying," she said to him. "My father is the liar. He told us the watch was here, but it isn't. I don't know where it is. I don't even believe there was a watch."

"Then what are you doing out here in the middle of the night?" the man asked.

If only Tanner could maneuver to get behind the man, then he might have a good chance to take him down without putting Josie at risk.

"Empty your pockets," the man demanded.

"Go to hell," Josie replied. Tanner stifled a groan. She was tempting fate! Mentally he begged her to comply with the man. Why was she arguing with him with a gun pointed at her chest?

"You can either empty your pockets yourself or I'll kill you and empty them for you."

Knowing he couldn't wait any longer, Tanner stepped out from behind the tree trunk. Everything happened in the snap of an eyelid. The man leaped forward, wrapped an arm around Josie's neck and shoved the gun under her chin as he stared at Tanner.

Josie's eyes were huge and seemed to plead with

him to do something—anything—but as long as the barrel of the man's gun kissed her slender throat they were at a standoff. There was no way Tanner could take a chance that the man wouldn't pull the trigger.

"Let her go," Tanner demanded.

The man laughed, an ugly, gravelly sound. "You sound like you think you're in control here. How about you drop your gun or I'll blow her head off."

"And then I'll shoot you and you'll be dead," Tanner countered, his nerves firing hot inside him.

The man cocked his head as if he were thinking about it. "That's true, but she'll still be dead, too. Are you willing to make that kind of a sacrifice?"

Not in a million years. Tanner weighed his options and realized he had none. The man could have shot her and killed her already. Tanner had to believe the last thing this man wanted was to commit cold-blooded murder.

"I'll put down my gun and you let her go," he finally said.

"How about you put your gun down and she gives me the watch," he replied. "Once I have the watch then the two of you can walk away from this without getting hurt. I don't want to hurt anyone, but I will if I have to."

"I told you…" Josie began but stopped as he shoved his gun barrel into her skin.

Tanner wanted to kill the man. He wanted to wrap his hands around his neck and squeeze until the life went out of him as he saw Josie wince with pain. But he couldn't do that. He couldn't do anything.

"Josie, it's not worth it," Tanner said desperately. "If you found the watch then give it to him now." He could only hope there was some sort of honor among thieves and once the man had the watch he'd let them both go.

Slowly, with great trepidation, he lowered his gun, bent down and placed it on the ground next to him. He straightened. "Your turn."

The man pulled the gun barrel from the bottom of her chin but kept his arm wrapped tight around her neck. "Now, give me that damn watch before something bad happens to both you and your boyfriend."

Tanner held his breath, hoping Josie had found the damn watch. He prayed she'd just give it to the man and this would all end here and now without anyone getting hurt.

Chapter 12

"Give it to me," the man shouted in her ear.

His arm tightened around her throat and Josie realized how much she wanted time to get to know her siblings better, how desperate she was to live her life.

Tanner stood as still as a statue, but his eyes pleaded with her to do what the man said. The last thing she wanted was to get him hurt, but she also didn't want to give the creep the watch. She wouldn't let him win.

"Damn you, girl, give it to me now," the man exclaimed.

Josie did just that. She pulled the small knife from her pocket, and with a prayer for strength, she plunged it into his upper thigh.

He screamed like an enraged bull and released

his hold on her. She slammed her fist into his hand and his gun fell to the ground. Tanner was on him in a hot minute.

With a roar, Tanner tackled him as she stumbled out of the way. She might have wounded the man, but she certainly hadn't hurt him enough to disable him.

She watched in horror as the two men grappled on the ground. They rolled over and over, crashing into the nearby bushes with first one man on top and then the other.

Her heart beat frantically and fear trembled through her body and tasted bitter in the back of her throat. Now her fear wasn't for herself, but for Tanner.

She'd been a reckless fool to come out here alone and now she'd put the man she loved in danger. Her fault; this was all her fault.

The two men rose to their feet, but the battle wasn't done. Tanner smashed his fist into the man's face and in turn received a blow to his chin that reeled him backward. "Tanner," she cried out.

Fists continued to fly and finally the terror that had kept her frozen in place snapped and she hurried over to where Tanner had placed his gun on the ground and she picked it up.

"Stop!" she screamed. "Stop it, both of you." She pointed the gun at them, but there was so much movement and so much shadowed darkness, she was afraid to fire it, terrified she would accidentally shoot Tanner.

Tears of frustration, of panicked horror, blurred

her vision. She should have given the man the watch when he'd first demanded it. She should have never let things get so out of control.

She cried out as the man punched Tanner in his eye. Tanner responded with an uppercut that threw the man backward on the ground. Tanner surged forward to attack once again, but the man grabbed his gun, got to his feet and quickly disappeared into the darkness of the night.

Tanner ran to her side and grabbed the gun from her. He pointed it in the direction the man had fled for several long moments and then he threw his arm around her shoulder. "Come on."

As they raced back Tanner kept his gun pointed all around them, before them and behind them. Her heart beat so hard it was as if the organ was splintering her ribs.

Blood flowed down the side of Tanner's face from a cut in his eyebrow and he breathed in harsh pants as they continued to run through the trees.

They exploded out of the woods and Tanner's horse awaited them. He jammed the gun into his holster, untied the horse and then quickly mounted.

"Give me your arm," he said urgently. "I'll pull you up and you swing your leg over to sit in the saddle behind me."

She moved close enough and he grabbed her by the upper arm, and through sheer brute strength he pulled her up and into the saddle.

She wrapped her arms tight around his waist as he

kicked his heels into the horse's sides and the horse shot forward. She squeezed her eyes tightly closed and hung on for dear life as they galloped across the dark landscape.

Tears chased each other down her cheeks as she buried her face in his back. She had no idea how badly he'd been hurt. The sight of his blood had terrified her. He'd been hit multiple times in the face and on his body.

Because of her.

Because she hadn't given up the watch immediately.

Why had he come after her in the first place? Why had he put himself at risk for her? And where were Lily and Leigh at this time of the night? Oh, God, why had she been so foolish?

"Don't shoot," Tanner yelled and reined in his horse.

She lifted her head to see they were nearly at the stable and a man on horseback had a rifle pointed in their direction.

"Tanner...is that you?"

"It's me, Steve." Tanner pulled his horse to a halt.

"Jeez, man, you nearly got your head shot off. What are you all doing out here in the middle of the night and what in the hell happened to your face?"

"It's a long story. We just want to get back inside the suite. I'll fill you in later." They continued toward the stable.

Once inside the dimly lit structure, he helped her

off the horse and pointed to a nearby wooden bench. "Sit. This will just take me a minute."

She didn't argue with him. Her legs didn't feel as if they could hold her up another minute. She sat on the bench and watched silently as he unsaddled his horse.

In the light the blood on his face looked even more horrifying, and a dark shadow had already appeared around his eye. He moved quickly, and when the horse was in a stall, he turned to her and gestured for her to stand up.

"I didn't mean to involve you in this," she finally said as they left the stable and headed toward the house.

"You were foolish to go out there by yourself."

She didn't reply. He was right, but she'd felt as if she'd had no choice. Once again hot tears filled her eyes. She'd just wanted to get the watch and go away from here.

She'd just wanted to fulfill her promise to her brothers and sister. Now the success of actually possessing the watch was tainted by the blood on Tanner's face. They didn't speak again as they walked to the staff door and then hurried toward his suite.

They stepped inside and Peggy sat up on the sofa and gasped in alarm. "Tanner! What happened to you?" She quickly got to her feet.

"I'm all right." He pulled up the bottom of his T-shirt and swiped at his face then grimaced as he saw the blood on the bottom of it. "I have a feeling it looks a lot worse than it is."

Peggy looked at him, then at Josie and then back at him once again. "Thank God you're both back relatively safe and sound. Now, what can I do to help?"

"Go to bed." He offered her a tight smile. "You've already done more than enough, Peggy. Go on to bed. We'll be fine." She eyed him dubiously. "Really, we can handle things from here," he said.

"Call me if I can do anything." She gazed at them worriedly, then shook her head and left the suite.

"Come into the bathroom and let me take a look at your eye," Josie said.

"I can take care of it myself." He turned and disappeared into his room.

Josie followed him into his bathroom. "Sit," she said and pointed to the stool. "You can be angry at me after I clean you up."

He scowled, but sank down with a weary sigh. She opened the counter beneath the sink and withdrew the same items he'd used when he'd cleaned the wound on her upper arm.

She used a warm washcloth to wash the blood from his face. His anger was a living, breathing third person in the small room. She ignored it as she began to clean the deep cut through his eyebrow.

She wanted to weep for his wounds. She wanted to fall to her knees and tell him how sorry she was about how everything had played out.

"You might need stitches," she said and fought back her tears. She feared he might forever carry a scar from this night forward.

"Just slap a couple of butterfly bandages on it and I'm sure it will be fine."

"You're going to have a black eye."

"You could have had a missing head," he retorted.

She bit her bottom lip and placed three of the small bandages on his cut. She stepped back from him. "I know you're angry—"

"Angry? Honest to God, I'm completely livid. Josie, you could have been killed out there." He stood and raked a hand through his hair, his eyes dark and hollow. "What on earth were you thinking?"

"I wasn't thinking, okay. I was just acting on emotion and knew it was time for me to leave here." She stalked out of the bathroom, aware of him following at her heels. A touch of anger rose up inside of her.

When she reached the living room, she turned back to face him. "I guess I was thinking that the only people I have in my life are my brothers and my sister and I wanted to get the watch for them. It was no longer any of your business, but thank you for making it your business and saving me once again."

Some of the anger left his eyes. "Did you find the watch?"

She reached in and pulled the item out of her pocket and held it out in her palm. "I did."

"Are you going to check to see if there is some sort of a treasure map inside it?"

She squeezed her hand closed over it and shook her head. "I'm going to call Trevor and ask him to come here first thing in the morning. We can check it out then—that is, if you'll let me stay here another night."

He frowned at her. "I wasn't the one who asked you to leave tonight."

"I thought it was the only choice I had after what happened between us." All the hurt of his rejection came rushing back. "Should we call the sheriff and report this?"

He swept a hand through his hair and appeared exhausted. "I really don't see any point in it unless you want to call him. We can't give him any more information than we did last time."

"I agree."

"I just don't want to fight anymore. It's late. You can sleep in my room. I'll stay in yours in case that creep decides to pull another break-in."

"He doesn't know I have it."

Once again Tanner's lips thinned and the fire of anger roared back into his eyes. "I hope it was worth it. I hope this somehow heals something inside of you. I wouldn't have been able to forgive myself if something happened to you. And now I need to take a shower and get some sleep."

As he went back into his bedroom, Josie sank down on the sofa and finally the last of her fear left her body on a shuddering shiver.

She didn't blame Tanner for being angry with her. She had been reckless in her quest to do something right, to please somebody. But her stubborn will had nearly gotten them both killed.

She closed her eyes with a weary sigh. Was this the end? When she handed the watch to her brother, would the madness finally stop?

Would she be able to go back to Granite Gulch and stop looking over her shoulders for the elusive bogeyman? And would she ever be able to forget she loved Tanner Grange?

He hoped getting the watch would heal something inside of her. She thought about his words. Did she need healing? Was there something broken inside of her? Maybe getting the watch was a last-ditch attempt of a little girl who still yearned for her father's love.

Her feelings for Matthew Colton would always be a mixture of hatred and love. She would always yearn for what she hadn't had from her father, just as she would always yearn for Tanner's love.

It didn't take long before he came back out of the bedroom. He was fully dressed in clean clothes and had his gun in one hand and a T-shirt in the other. "I'm assuming your suitcase is in your car." She nodded and he tossed her the shirt. "You can sleep in that for tonight and I definitely think it's time to call it a night. Good night, Josie."

There were still so many things she wanted to say to him, but she settled for a good-night. She watched him as he walked down the hallway and disappeared into the small bedroom she had vacated what felt like a lifetime ago.

She pulled herself up off the sofa and went into his bedroom. She went into the bathroom and stripped off her clothes and then stepped into a hot shower.

The water warmed the last of the chill that had encased her body since the moment the man had appeared with his gun. She braced her hands against the glass enclosure and allowed the water to wash over her.

It was done.

She'd accomplished what she'd come here for and what she needed now was her big brother to come here and decipher any secret the watch might hold. Then he could follow her back to Granite Gulch. She'd feel safe with him tailing her. Just as she'd felt in Tanner's arms.

She shook her head to dislodge any thoughts of Tanner. The drama that had played out in the woods tonight hadn't changed his mind about her. He hadn't saved her and then taken her into his arms and told her the close call had made him realize just how much he loved her.

It was definitely done and over.

She got out of the shower, dried off and then pulled Tanner's T-shirt over her head. Sitting on the edge of the bed, she grabbed her cell phone and punched in the number that would speed-dial Trevor.

She hated that it was so late, but she wanted—needed—him here first thing in the morning.

"Josie, what's wrong?" His voice was filled with urgent concern.

She started to speak and then burst into tears.

Tanner lay in the bed that smelled of peaches and all things Josie and knew this was a night where he'd find no sleep. Myriad emotions flooded his brain as the hours ticked by toward morning.

The cut on his eyebrow throbbed, along with body parts he hadn't even known he possessed, but that wasn't the pain that would keep him awake.

Only now could he fully take in the absolute horror of seeing the man's gun pressed against Josie's throat. Only now, knowing she was safe, could he fully process how close she'd been to being killed.

What if he hadn't awakened when he had? What if he hadn't decided to go down the hallway to check on his girls? What if he hadn't wanted a single peek at Josie while she slept and realized she was gone?

What if he hadn't gotten there in time? So many things could have gone so very wrong, and as he cataloged them all in his mind, a harsh chill suffused him, a chill that remained with him for hours.

It was good her brother was coming tomorrow, he told himself. It would be good for her to have the emotional support of her big brother.

FBI Agent Trevor Colton would make sure she got home safe and sound, and hopefully the encounter in the woods would be the last of it and she could truly get on with her life.

A life without him.

A new pain pierced through his heart. He would always remember his time with Josie with a smile on his face, with a sweet warmth in his heart and, yes, with a fire in his blood.

The girls were young enough that within a couple of weeks or so they would have no memories of the loving, beautiful woman who had been in their lives briefly. They wouldn't remember her tickles, her laughter or her kisses.

He would remember. He would remember it all. He had a feeling it would take a very long time for him to stop thinking about Josie Colton.

He frowned. He had plenty of vacation time built up. He'd tell Whitney he needed to take that time and find a new nanny. In the meantime, he knew Peggy would help out if necessary and he wasn't going to hire anyone too quickly.

Josie had been a handy convenience. She'd loved his babies and they had loved her. She'd been good at taking care of them. She'd been patient and had been teaching them manners and had used discipline with a firm, but loving hand.

Surely that was part of his attraction to Josie. Just as he didn't believe she really loved him, he didn't believe he could possibly be in love with her.

I don't love her, he told himself firmly. *And even if I did, I still have to let her go.*

He must have fallen asleep, for he awakened with dawn's light just beginning to filter into the bedroom. A new day… The day he'd say a final good-bye to Josie.

He slid out of bed and crept across the hall into the guest bathroom. He turned on the light and closed the door and then stared at his reflection in the mirror. The good news was the butterfly bandages seemed to be holding. A faint purple bruise formed a half-moon beneath his eye but it wasn't as bad as he'd expected it to be.

He still felt as if he'd been run over by a truck, but the muscle strains would ease up, and all in all, he would survive. He just needed to get through today. He just needed to get past the sight of Josie's car leaving the ranch.

After carefully washing his face, he left the bathroom and went down the hallway to the kitchen, where he put a pot of coffee on to brew.

As he waited for the coffee, he moved to the window and stared outside. The sun had broken free of the horizon and promised another hot, cloudless day.

Eldridge was still missing, there were still too many suspects and now Josie would be gone. He had a feeling that life at the Colton Valley Ranch would never be the same again.

He managed to drink a half a cup of coffee before he heard Lily calling from the nursery. He hurried in to attend to them, not wanting them to awaken Josie. She'd had a late night, and in any case, they weren't her job anymore.

Lily frowned at the sight of him, her gaze lingering on his eye. "Daddy-love…boo-boo?"

"It's okay. Daddy is okay." He gave her a reassuring smile.

Lily reached up and placed her hand on his eye. "Daddy-love boo-boo. All better!"

"All better," he agreed as his heart swelled. These two girls were all he needed in his life. He didn't need anything else. He just had to stay focused on being the best father in the world and that would be enough for him and hopefully that would be enough for them.

Fifteen minutes later he carried both of the girls into the kitchen, where he deposited them in their high chairs. They jabbered their usual secret language to each other as he cut up a banana for them to eat while he cooked them some eggs.

The only thing missing in the kitchen was Josie's happy mood that had been bright enough to fill the room with sunshine even on a dark and cloudy day.

He'd just gotten out the eggs from the fridge when Josie came into the room.

"Josie-love, kiss Lily," Lily demanded.

"Kiss Leigh, Josie-love," Leigh said.

Josie walked over and gave them each a kiss on the forehead and then turned and looked at him. She offered him a smile but the gesture didn't quite reach the simmering darkness in her eyes. "Good morning."

"How did you sleep?" he asked.

"In fits and starts," she replied, then walked over to the cabinet and pulled down a coffee cup. "What about you?"

"I think I got about an hour's worth." He broke two eggs into an awaiting bowl and then popped two pieces of bread into the toaster. "Did you call your brother last night?"

"Yes, and he should be here sometime between eight and nine this morning." She poured her coffee and then sat at the island. "I told him we could all look at the watch together."

"All? As in you and me and Trevor?" He shook his head. "It's really not my business if something is inside the watch. You don't have to include me," he protested. The last thing he wanted was to intrude in any way.

"Aren't you curious?"

"Absolutely," he admitted. The toast popped up and he turned back to the counter to butter and cut it into squares for the twins. Once that was accomplished, he refilled his coffee cup and joined her at the island, the scrambled eggs momentarily on hold.

"You more than earned the right to know what you fought for," she said. She frowned as her gaze focused on his eye.

"I wasn't fighting for the watch."

She looked down into her coffee. "I realize that and I'll never be able to thank you enough for all you've done for me while I've been here. I'll never be able to thank you for saving my life on more than one occasion."

"And I can't thank you enough for stepping up to fill in as nanny to my girls. I owe you wages and I'll see to it that you have a check before you leave here today."

Her gaze flew up to meet his and she scowled. "I don't want your money, Tanner."

"But you've earned it," he protested.

She shook her head vehemently. "Having Lily and Leigh in my life for a little while was more than payment enough. Consider that we're square."

The girls began to babble to each other at the sound of their names and for a few minutes he and Josie sat in what should have been a companionable silence, but wasn't.

Despite the overall relatively pleasant tone to their conversation, so far there was a distinct underlying tension in the air between them. Tanner knew it was born out of the conversation they'd had last night, before she'd left the suite, before she'd put her life at risk.

Her words of love still rang in his ears no matter how hard he tried to dismiss them, and he was certain his words of rejection still clanged in her ears.

He couldn't fix it. No matter what she said, no matter what she did, it wouldn't change his conviction that he had to let her go. It was the right thing to do for both of them.

"How about I fix us some breakfast?" He was

suddenly desperate for something to do besides sit in silence next to her.

"You can cook?"

"I can manage an omelet and some toast," he replied. "I was just getting ready to scramble some eggs for the girls before you came in."

"Scrambled eggs sound good," she agreed.

He slid off the stool and busied himself gathering the rest of the ingredients for the meal. As he worked, Josie chatted with the girls, making them laugh with delight over and over again.

This was what life would be like with Josie…sweet laughter served with breakfast and hot passion at night. He poured the egg mixture into the awaiting pan and shoved away the very thought of "what if?"

He was thankful for the girls' presence later as he and Josie ate their breakfast in relative silence. He grieved for the easy conversations he and Josie had always shared, for the sense of partnership that had existed between them almost from the moment they had met.

There was no question that things had felt natural and right between them up until she'd told him she loved him. Only then had cold reality slapped him in the face.

Tanner was cleaning up the kitchen and Josie had moved to the living-room floor with the twins when a knock sounded on the door. He looked at the clock on the oven. Just before eight.

"I'll get it," he said, not wanting to take any

chances. Just because they were expecting Trevor Colton didn't necessarily mean he was the person knocking.

As soon as he opened the door, despite the differences in their ages, he instantly saw the resemblance between Trevor and Josie. They both had rich, dark hair, and although Trevor's eyes were dark and intense, they were the same shape as Josie's.

"Tanner Grange?"

Tanner nodded. "And I'm assuming you're Josie's oldest brother, Trevor." Tanner opened the door wider. "Please come in."

Josie got up off the floor and threw herself into Trevor's arms, and the two of them hugged in obvious affection. "Are you all right?" Trevor took a step back from her and then looked at Tanner. "She was a bit shaky when I spoke to her last night."

"We were both a little bit shaky last night," Tanner agreed and reached up self-consciously to touch his eye.

"I hope the other guy looks worse," Trevor said.

"Yeah, so do I," Tanner replied ruefully. "Unfortunately, he ran off before I could check."

"We're all okay this morning," Josie said as if not wanting to think about the night before. "Now, let me introduce you to two of the cutest little girls you'll ever meet in your life."

Trevor grinned teasingly at his sister. "I might think they are the cutest kids on the planet for now, but that will change when Jocelyn has my child."

As Trevor bent down to talk to the twins, Tanner wondered exactly what Josie had told her brother about him…about them. When she'd spoken to him the night before, had she told him that Tanner had broken her heart?

"They're definitely cuties," Trevor said.

"Thanks." Tanner gestured him to a seat on the sofa and Josie sat next to him.

Tanner sat in the chair and for the next few minutes he and Trevor exchanged pleasantries. "Too bad Ethan can't see this spread," Trevor said to Josie and then looked at Tanner. "Ethan is one of our brothers. He has a small cattle ranch ten miles outside of Granite Gulch."

"He wouldn't be able to imagine having a ranch this size," Josie replied. Her eyes held a new warmth as she gazed at Trevor, a warmth Tanner perversely wished he saw again in her eyes when she gazed at him. But he'd doused that heat with his stark rejection of the love she believed she had for him.

After a few minutes of talking about family members, their father's dire physical condition and the events of the night before, Trevor cut to the chase. "You've got the watch?"

Josie nodded and dug into her pocket. She held the pocket watch out to her brother. "Maybe it doesn't have anything inside of it. Maybe it really just has sentimental value to Father."

Trevor released a low, dry laugh. "Do you really

believe anything has sentimental value to that man?" He turned the watch over and then looked at Tanner.

"Do you have a little knife or a screwdriver I can use to pry the back off?" he asked.

Tanner got up and went to the drawer in the kitchen that held spare screws, batteries of different sizes and a variety of other junk items. He found a small screwdriver, and Trevor and Josie moved to the island.

"Up, Josie-love," Lily said and wrapped her arms around Josie's knees. Josie picked her up and at the same time Leigh held out her arms toward Tanner.

He held her close and once again tension filled the air as Trevor used the screwdriver to pry off the back of the rusted watch.

It took him several tries before he succeeded. The back popped off and he released a small gasp. "There's something here." He used his fingers and pulled out a small piece of folded, yellowed paper.

Tanner found himself holding his breath as Trevor gingerly opened the piece of paper. If this really was a map to buried money, he had a feeling Josie's brothers and sister could use it to better their lives.

He wished that for them…for her. They'd all been handed such a raw deal by their father and what his actions had done to their family. They deserved whatever they found and he hoped it was a million dollars.

But from what Josie had told him about her father, he wouldn't be surprised if the note inside was some kind of a sick joke.

Trevor stared down at the paper and then looked up at Josie, his dark eyes glittering with excitement. "Josie girl, it's a map."

Chapter 13

Josie set Lily back down on the floor and leaned over the paper with the faint ink drawings. Her heart beat with excitement, an excitement that waned slightly as she tried to make sense of what she was looking at.

There was a squiggly line that ran up the left side of the map and what appeared to be three humps and some sort of building in the upper right corner. An arrow pointed to the center hump with the infamous *X* marking a spot directly in front. A small compass had been drawn in the lower right-hand side.

"This isn't any help," she finally said and looked up at her brother. "We don't even know where this place is."

Trevor's eyebrows pulled together in a frown. "If

those humps are mountains, then there's no way the treasure is anywhere around here. And if it's not here then who knows where it might be."

Tanner placed Leigh on the floor. "Do you mind if I take a look?"

"Be my guest," Trevor replied and pushed the paper closer to him.

Josie watched as he bent over the island top. There was no question that things had been awkward between them this morning and each awkward moment had ached inside of her.

She'd gone through so much in her life, but nothing had prepared her for this kind of heartbreak. She'd survived foster care and a drug lord's wrath and come out stronger on the other side, but now she felt broken by a handsome cowboy and his two little girls.

"I think I know this place," Tanner said tentatively. "This squiggly line on the left looks like the stream on the property, and it's possible those humps aren't mountains, but they're old grain silos toward the back of the property. We don't use them anymore, but twenty years ago they would have probably been some of the few structures on the property."

He looked up at Josie and then at Trevor. "If I'm right then I can take you there."

Josie gazed up at her brother. His eyes once again gleamed with barely suppressed excitement. "It's worth a shot, right?"

"Definitely," Trevor agreed.

"I just need to get Peggy here to watch the girls.

I'll take them into the nursery and make the call there. Lily and Leigh, let's go find some toys."

Josie watched as he disappeared down the hallway, the pink-and-purple-clad twins toddling behind him. Once again a shaft of pain shot straight through her heart.

"Whoa," Trevor said in a whisper. Josie turned to look at him. He gazed at her with a knowing glint in his eyes. "You're in love with that man."

Her first impulse was to deny, but as she opened her mouth to do just that, unexpected tears blurred her vision. She quickly blinked them away and shook her head. "It doesn't matter what I feel about him and it doesn't matter how he feels about me. The bottom line is that he thinks I'm too young for him and I haven't experienced enough real life."

"Enough real life?" Trevor released a small dry laugh. "I'd say you've experienced far too much real life already."

"I tried to tell him that, but it didn't matter. He thinks I'm too young to know what I feel, to know how I want to spend my life." A hollow wind blew through her. "I'm just ready now to finish things up here and go back to Granite Gulch and figure things out by myself."

"You know you have our support, Josie." Trevor's gaze was so warm and caring. "All of us will be there for you no matter what you decide to do with the rest of your life."

She smiled. "It's been a long time coming that

we're finally all together again." Her smile fell away. "Have you heard how Father is doing?"

Trevor's eyes darkened. "I spoke to the warden last night to get an update. As I told you on the phone, he's failing fast and they don't think he has much time left...probably only a couple of days."

"Then I guess it's good we can get the watch to him sometime tomorrow."

"I have a feeling he won't be happy to discover his little map has been found."

"He told us he wanted it for sentimental reasons. Besides, what difference does it make to him? He can't very well go retrieve his hidden fortune. At least he'll die with it in his hands."

"And he won't need the map in hell," Trevor added flatly.

Josie nodded, unsurprised by Trevor's cool tone. Trevor had kept himself relatively emotionally uninvolved with their father. Maybe it was because as the eldest child Trevor had more memories of their mother than anyone, or perhaps it was because in his capacity as an FBI profiler he'd learned to maintain a professional objectivity when dealing with criminals like Matthew Colton.

"Peggy should be here in just a few minutes," Tanner said as he came back up the hallway. He'd strapped on his holster and with his darkened eye he looked slightly dangerous.

"Are you expecting trouble?" Trevor asked with a pointed look at Tanner's gun.

"Since Eldridge's kidnapping I never go out on the property without a gun on my hip. And then there is the creep from last night."

"You gave him a pretty good beating," Josie said. "Hopefully he ran for the hills." She touched under her chin, remembering the cold, hard bite of the man's gun against her skin. It had been one of the most terrifying moments she'd ever experienced.

"We hoped that last time and still he turned up again like a cockroach," Tanner replied.

"I wish I would have enough information to identify him and get him behind bars," Trevor replied grimly.

"That makes three of us," Tanner said.

A knock sounded at the door. "That will be Peggy." Tanner strode across the room and opened the door and Peggy swept in.

She stopped in her tracks at the sight of Trevor. "Well, well, isn't this a lucky day for an old woman. Not one piece of eye candy, but two."

Josie was amused to see not only Tanner's cheeks blush with faint color, but her brother's as well. "Peggy, this is my brother Trevor," she said. "And this is Peggy, Tanner's right-hand woman when it comes to taking care of his daughters."

Josie shoved away the yearning that filled her. She'd hoped she would be Tanner's right-hand woman through the rest of his life, but that hope had been shattered.

She couldn't think about that now. She had to stay

focused on the reality that within a couple of hours or so, she'd be gone from here forever.

"The girls are in the nursery," Tanner said to Peggy.

"I'll head back there now." With a nod and a coy smile at Trevor, Peggy scurried down the hallway.

"Are we ready to head out?" Tanner asked.

Trevor picked up the map from the island. "Ready." Together they all left the suite.

"We'll take one of the ranch pickups," Tanner said as they stepped outside into the hot morning sunshine. "You two wait here. I'll be right back." He headed in the direction of the barn where he'd retrieved the shovel on the first day she'd arrived at the ranch.

She hadn't known on that day just how deeply the handsome, blond cowboy would dig into her heart. When she'd followed him out of the parlor on that very first day, she'd had no clue that he and his daughters would grow to mean so much to her.

"You okay?" Trevor asked.

She raised her chin. "I'm fine. What do you think we're going to find at that *X*?"

"I hope we find all the money Matthew ever stole," Trevor replied. "That's only if Tanner is right and the map really is of this property. If it isn't, then we might never find where any treasure is buried."

"And we have to be okay with that," she said.

"I'll be okay when this chapter is closed and we can all move forward with our lives."

The sound of an engine filled the air and Tanner

appeared driving a black, king-cab pickup. He pulled up next to them and Trevor got into the passenger seat while Josie got in the back. She was grateful to see Tanner had thought to throw a couple of shovels into the bed of the truck.

"Buckle up," Tanner instructed. Josie quickly buckled the seat belt and then he took off. Josie fought for breath as the hot wind from Trevor's open window slapped her in the face.

Would this be where they found their father's ill-gotten spoils? Would this somehow be the final closure to Matthew Colton's crimes of so long ago?

There was a little part of her that would grieve the loss of a father, but there was very little mourning in her heart for the real Matthew Colton. He'd spent so much of his life causing pain to others, even taking pleasure in tormenting and manipulating his own children. As horrible as it sounded, his death would be a relief.

She was saying goodbye to the men who could have, who should have loved her. Her father should have loved her and Tanner could have if only he wasn't so hung up about the difference in their ages.

She shoved these thoughts out of her head and reached up to grab a handle over the door as they trekked across rougher terrain. She fought against a shiver as on their left they passed the thick woods where they could have been killed the night before.

In the light of day she was even more appalled at the foolhardy decision she'd made to go out and attempt to retrieve the watch all alone. If Tanner hadn't come to her rescue, she could have very possibly been killed and her body wouldn't have been found until Tanner had awakened this morning and realized she was gone.

They passed men on horseback who waved, obviously recognizing Tanner behind the wheel of the ranch vehicle. Outbuildings flashed by in the blink of an eye as they headed farther and farther away from the main house.

She sat forward eagerly as in the distance she saw the rise of three old grain elevators. The large round cylinders were obviously abandoned and aged to a dull gray.

The wooden building next to them was scarcely a building anymore. The windows had been broken and some of the roof had fallen in and the entire structure listed heavily to one side.

Was this it? Was this really the place? Certainly it appeared to match what was on the map. A thrum of excitement filled her stomach. Everything else had gone so terribly wrong. She just wanted this one thing to be right.

Tanner pulled their vehicle parallel to the silos, but about twenty yards away, and cut the engine. "I don't want to park any closer because of falling and broken concrete," he said. "We haven't used these silos in years. I don't think anyone ever comes out this far on the property anymore."

"This definitely looks like the place on the map," Trevor replied, echoing Josie's thoughts.

"Then the next step is to dig," Tanner said.

They all got out of the truck and Tanner grabbed the shovels. Together they began the walk across the burned grass and tall weeds toward the silos.

"I'll bet finding a fortune will help your family out a lot," Tanner said.

"Emotionally it will definitely be satisfying," Trevor replied. "But none of us will see any financial gain from this. There's no way to know how to get the money back into the hands it was originally taken from, so whatever we find will be donated to charity."

"That's nice of you," Tanner said.

"It's the right thing to do," Josie replied. "It's tainted money. None of us want anything to do with it. There are several great charities in Granite Gulch that could use a good windfall."

"I really appreciate you helping us out with this," Trevor said to Tanner. "And I definitely appreciate you taking care of Josie while she's been here."

Josie stared at Tanner. He didn't meet her gaze. "No problem," he said. "It's been a pleasure to spend time with her."

The lukewarm words only hurt her more than she already had been hurt. *A pleasure to spend time with her*, like she was a favorite aunt who had come for a visit. She couldn't wait to dig up whatever treasure there might be and then run before he could unconsciously inflict any more hurt.

They reached the front of the center silo and Tanner dug the shovel into the dirt about three feet away from the structure. "Should we start right here?"

"You aren't starting anywhere," Trevor replied. "You've done enough in getting us here. There's no way I'm going to let you do the digging."

Tanner flashed him a quick smile and stepped back from the shovel. "Knock yourself out," he said.

A gunshot exploded, the bullet pinging off the silo mere inches from Josie's head. "Get down," Tanner yelled just before he tackled her to the ground.

Tanner yanked his gun from his holster at the same time he covered Josie's body with his own. He turned his head to see that Trevor had hit the ground as well.

"The shooter is over there in the trees," Trevor shouted. The trees were on the other side of their vehicle and provided just enough cover to hide a man with a gun.

And they had no cover at all.

Tanner cursed beneath his breath as another bullet kicked up the dirt just in front of them. He curled around the small woman beneath him as she gasped in fear, his need to protect her foremost in his mind. Even though he knew it was impossible, he swore he could feel her heartbeat fluttering frantically against his own chest.

There was no question in his mind it was the same man from the night before. He must have been watching the suite and had tailed them here. Damn, if only Tanner had managed to somehow permanently take out the man last night.

Tanner had hoped the man didn't have any killer blood in his veins. After all, he hadn't shot them during the previous two encounters even though he'd had ample opportunity. But the cold, hard fact now was that he was obviously shooting to kill.

Yet another bullet puffed up dust far too close to where they were on the ground. "We need to get to cover," he yelled to Trevor.

"Take her and get into the building. I'll cover you both," Trevor replied. "On the count of three. One… two…three."

Trevor rose to a crouching position and fired off a volley of shots toward the trees. At the same time Tanner jumped up and grabbed Josie from the ground. He threw an arm around her shoulder in an effort to shield her as they raced for the structure next to the silos.

He guided her through the open doorway. "Get on the ground," he said tersely to Josie and then turned to fire his gun toward the woods, hoping to provide adequate cover for Trevor to join them in the relative safety of the building.

Trevor ran inside and Tanner breathed a sigh of relief. He moved to the window opening, broken glass crunching under his feet, as Trevor remained just inside the doorway.

Adrenaline pumped hard and fast through Tanner's veins as he stared out in the distance, looking for any movement that might give the exact location of the shooter.

He glanced at Josie, who was crouched next to the window, her eyes wide with fear. God, he'd seen her this way too many times. And as always, what he wanted to do most of all was sweep her away from here, make sure terror never darkened her eyes again.

And in this moment, with the acrid scent of gunpowder in the air, he recognized the undeniable fact that he was completely in love with Josie Colton.

A volley of bullets slammed into the building, splintering wood on the outside but thankfully not piercing through the thick wood to the inside.

Then silence.

A minute ticked by…then two…then three. The silence was heavy and thick with dreadful anticipation. At least when the man was shooting at them they had an idea of his whereabouts. The silence told them nothing.

"He didn't just go away," Tanner said after several more minutes had passed. "He's come after the watch twice before. He's definitely determined to get your father's treasure."

Trevor's features were taut, his dark eyes narrowed as he looked at his sister and then back at

Tanner. "I don't know about you, but I didn't bring enough ammunition for a long standoff."

"And we have no idea what kind of ammunition supply this creep has," Tanner replied with a new squeeze of his gut.

"Peek out that window and see if he's still in the same place," Trevor said and then stepped into the open doorway. Tanner slid his head around the side of the window to peer outside.

Several shots rang out. Trevor hit the floor and rolled backward to safety as Josie released a scream. "Are you okay?" Tanner asked Trevor. Trevor nodded and got to his feet.

"I saw him behind the big oak tree right behind the truck," Tanner said. "We're sitting ducks in here. He can keep us pinned down until we run out of bullets."

"If you can provide me some cover, I'll sneak out of here and try to get behind him, where hopefully I can get a jump on him," Trevor said.

"No, Trevor," Josie protested frantically. "It's too dangerous. Just stay here. Maybe somebody from the ranch will hear the shots and come to help us."

"Is that possible?" Trevor asked Tanner.

"I don't know," Tanner replied truthfully. "We're quite some distance from the house, and as far as I know, none of the cowboys have any reason to come out here. I don't think we can wait for anyone to ride to our rescue and we can't call for help because there's no cell phone service out here."

Trevor's dark brows pulled into a frown. "As far as we know, it's just one creep." He walked toward the back of the building, where a doorway provided an easy exit.

He faced Tanner once again. "You make sure nothing happens to my sister." He offered a grim smile. "We haven't had her in our life long enough yet to want to get rid of her."

"Trevor!" This time Josie's cry was filled with tearful emotion.

Trevor held Tanner's gaze. "When I go out, give me five seconds and then shoot a few shots to provide a bit of a distraction."

"Got it." Tanner moved into place at the window and then watched as Trevor disappeared out the back of the building. He waited five seconds and then fired out the window, garnering a volley of return fire that assured him the man hadn't moved from his position.

Then silence once again. Silence except for the sound of Josie softly sobbing.

"He'll be all right, Josie," Tanner said softly. "He's a trained FBI agent. He knows what he's doing."

"He's all I have. My brothers and sister are all I have in the world. I can't bear the thought of losing any of them."

How he wanted to comfort her. How desperately he wanted to crouch down next to her and pull her into his arms, but he couldn't.

He needed to keep his attention focused outside

and he feared in touching her, in pulling her into a comforting embrace, he'd only give her mixed signals.

Instead he kept his gaze out the window, not wanting the shooter to creep up on them and take them by surprise. At the moment Josie's safety was far more important than any reassurance he might give to her.

Once again the silence grew to stifling proportions as minutes ticked by. Tanner focused on the large tree where he'd seen movement before. Was the man still there?

And where was Trevor? There wasn't a lot of cover the FBI agent could use, and it would take time for him to get behind the man. Did they have that kind of time?

Tanner did a mental calculation and realized he had only four bullets left. If the man did a full-out assault, he'd probably win. The thought dried Tanner's mouth and a rivulet of perspiration trickled down the center of his back.

And still the silence continued. As the sun moved higher in the sky, the building was quickly becoming an inferno and they had no water. It wouldn't take long for that to become an issue as well.

"We should have known he'd still be out there." Josie had stopped crying and her voice was a little stronger than it had been before. "We should have anticipated he wouldn't just give up and go away."

"You're right," Tanner replied.

"I should have just left here yesterday when I had the watch. My father could have been buried with the stupid treasure map and that would have been the end of it. We all just wanted a chance to give back a little bit of what our father took."

"And that's still going to happen," he replied with as much assurance as he could muster, although with every minute Trevor was gone, tension twisted tighter in Tanner's stomach.

What was happening? Would Trevor manage to neutralize the threat or would the man somehow manage to overtake Trevor? If Trevor got hurt would they even know it? Dammit, what was taking so long?

Tanner didn't even want to think about something bad happening to Josie's brother. She'd only recently had a chance to reunite with him.

"I should have never come here," Josie said. "We all should have just let the watch stay buried. It was stupid of us to all be manipulated into giving in to his wishes."

A gunshot rang out and Josie jumped to her feet, her eyes huge with terror. "Trevor?" Her lips trembled with his name.

Tanner stared out the window, his heart pounding fast and furious. He released a sigh of relief as Trevor stepped out into the clearing with the familiar man at gunpoint in front of him.

"Trevor is okay. He's got him. He's got him, Josie." He grabbed her by the arm and together they left the building and ran toward Trevor.

As they approached, the man's curses filled the air.

"Let me go, damn you," he exclaimed to Trevor, who held him in the back by his belt.

"That's not going to happen," Trevor replied. "You have any rope in that pickup?" he asked Tanner.

"I'm sure we can find something to truss him up like a turkey and take him to Sheriff Watkins," Tanner replied. "He'll be facing charges of attempted murder, among other things."

"His name is Walt Cleaver. His wallet was in his back pocket. I imagine if I run him through the system there are probably some outstanding warrants to answer to," Trevor said.

"I didn't do nothing wrong," Walt yelled. "I have as much right to Matthew's money as anyone." He glared at Josie. "You bitch, all you had to do last night was give me the watch."

Trevor cuffed him on the side of his head. "Watch your mouth."

"I'll just get that rope and see if I can find something to shove in his mouth while I'm at it," Tanner said, wanting nothing more than to smash his fist into Walt's face.

Minutes later Walt was tied up. They tied his wrists and ankles, and he sat in the cab where he was out of the sun.

The three of them headed back to where the shovel was still stuck in the dirt. "Now, let's see what we find." Trevor began to dig.

The morning hours slipped away as Tanner and Trevor took turns digging in the hard ground. The sun beat down on them as they widened the search area, unsure exactly what they might find. The only sound was an occasional curse and shout from Walt.

Josie stood silently by and more than once Tanner felt her gaze lingering on him. Whether this dig ended in success or not, he knew she would be leaving the Colton Valley Ranch before nightfall.

He shoved back the rise of emotions he didn't want to feel, that he didn't want to analyze. At that moment Trevor's shovel thrust clanged against something in the ground.

Both Tanner and Josie stepped closer to the hole as Trevor carefully used the end of the shovel to move dirt away from what appeared to be a small tin box.

"That's got to be it," Josie said with excitement. "It's right where the map said it would be."

Even though Tanner had no real vested interest in what they found, excitement thrummed in his veins as well. Trevor threw the shovel aside and crouched down to grab the metal box that could only hold Matthew's treasure.

"This is it, Josie girl," Trevor said as he cradled the box in his hands. He smiled at Tanner. "Thank you for risking your life so we can all have a little bit of closure."

"Just open it," Josie replied with a small laugh of impatience.

"I feel like there should be a drumroll or something," Trevor replied.

The light mood was a welcome relief after what they had all just gone through. "I'm with Josie," Tanner said. "Just open it."

It wasn't locked, but it took Trevor a couple of hard pulls before he managed to open the rusty lid. Inside were three old cans of soda, several sticks of beef jerky, a pocketknife and a wad of money.

Trevor said nothing. He handed the money to Josie, who counted it. "Sixty-five dollars," she said flatly. "We all risked our lives for a lousy sixty-five dollars and a couple of cans of old soda." She started to laugh, the sound holding just a little touch of hysteria.

"We should have known," Trevor said in disgust. He took the cash from Josie and shoved it back in the box, then put the lid back on top. "Let's get out of here."

Tanner tried to think of something to say that would take away the sting of their father's obvious manipulation, but no words came to him.

He was grateful when Trevor slung an arm around Josie's shoulder in an obvious effort to console her. Tanner didn't have that right.

As he walked behind the brother and sister, he wondered how many minutes, how many hours before he had to say a final goodbye to Josie Colton.

Chapter 14

The next three hours were sheer torture for Josie. They called Troy and he arrived to take statements and custody of Walt.

As Trevor and Tanner explained to the sheriff everything that had happened during the morning, all Josie could think about was that she and Tanner had faced yet another dire situation together and still he hadn't fallen to his knees and proclaimed his love for her.

When Troy had left with the prisoner, they all returned to the suite, where the twins' loving greeting only splintered her heart even more. Tanner put them down for their afternoon nap and then returned to the living room, where he and Trevor chewed over all that had happened.

Had she truly mistaken Tanner's love for her? Had she only fantasized the softness of his gaze when it had lingered on her so many times over the past couple of weeks? Had she misheard the depth of caring in his tone of voice, in their shared laughter?

Had he only pretended to be on fire when they kissed? When they had made love, had it really been passion without love? Had it just been sex?

It would be so much easier if she believed all that in her heart. But she didn't. She knew with a woman's instinct that he loved her. He was just too stubborn to embrace it. He was just too scared to believe in it.

Although she'd been disappointed by the treasure that wasn't there, none of that mattered now. It was time to say goodbye to Tanner and his girls.

"Tanner, it was a pleasure to meet you," Trevor said as the two men shook hands. It was after four and time for them to get home to Granite Gulch. Trevor turned and looked at Josie. "Are you ready?"

"Could you give me a few minutes?" she asked. She couldn't walk away without giving it one last try, without one final fight for her future.

"Sure. I'll just wait for you out by the cars." Trevor left the suite.

The twins were still napping, and when she turned to look at Tanner, his features held the same kind of yearning that burned in her heart. The naked, raw emotion was there only a moment and then was masked by a pleasant but distant smile.

"At least you aren't sneaking off like a thief in

the middle of the night so that we can say a proper goodbye," he said.

"I don't want to say a proper goodbye. I don't want to say goodbye at all."

His eyes darkened. "Josie, please don't make this hard."

"But it should be hard for you to turn your back on love." She took a step closer to him. "Tanner, I've never been so sure of anything in my life as I am about our love for each other. I want to raise your baby girls as if they're my own."

Her heart beat a little quicker and she took another step closer to him. "Tanner, I want to give you more children and spend my days and nights with you. You're the man I want to grow old with."

"Josie," he said softly. She didn't realize she was crying until he reached out and gently swiped the tears from her cheeks. His touch caused an ache inside her and stirred a tiny ray of hope.

She gazed up at him, her love a piercing pain only he could stop. "Josie," he repeated.

His hands lingered for a long moment on the sides of her face and then he stepped backward and dropped his hands to his sides. "You're so beautiful, not just on the outside, but on the inside as well. Go home, Josie. The last thing you need is to be dealing with me and my daughters. You're too young to be burdened with dirty diapers and temper tantrums."

"Burdened?" She stared at him incredulously. "For every diaper I change, I get a kiss and a hug. For every tear I dry, I get back so much love it fills me up. They would never be a burden. They're a gift. I want to be your wife. I want to be their mother."

He stuck his hands in his pockets and appeared completely unmoved by her words. "You haven't had time to figure out what you're good at, what you really want to do for the rest of your life."

"I know what I'm good at," she replied fervently. "I'm good at loving you and Lily and Leigh." Tears once again leaped to her eyes and she angrily swiped them away. "I survived having a serial killer for a father and foster care and the wrath of a drug lord. Don't you understand I'm old with life experience?"

"Josie, go home and build a wonderful life for yourself. Before long you'll find some nice young man and you'll forget all about your time here. You'll forget all about me."

"You're wrong," she replied flatly. Any hope she might have momentarily entertained died in the fathomless depths of his eyes, in his body posture that spoke of stark, cold rejection. "You'll tell the girls I said goodbye?" A new grief pressed hot tears behind her eyelids, but before they could fall, she murmured a goodbye and then turned and left the suite.

It was over. No matter what she believed in her heart, in her soul, she couldn't force Tanner to believe in her love for him, in his love for her.

The late afternoon sunshine half blinded her as she left the house and headed toward her car. Trevor's car was parked next to her and he got out of his as she approached.

"Everything all right?" he asked.

"Fine," she lied. "It's time to get home. Thankfully I don't have to worry about any more danger where the watch is concerned."

"Speaking of…" Trevor pulled the old watch out of his pocket and handed it to her. "You're the one who got it for him. You can take it to him tomorrow or whenever you decide."

Josie thought about going to the Blackthorn County Prison to see Matthew. She would give him the watch and then she'd never go to see him again. The little girl who had needed her father no longer needed him. "I'll take it to him tomorrow."

Trevor gave her a quick hug. "I'm so proud of you, Josie. We're all so proud of you."

On any other day, in any other circumstance, his words would have warmed her. But with the cold wind of heartache blowing through her, she didn't think she would ever be completely warm again.

Within minutes she was in her car with Trevor following behind her in his. She managed to hold it together through the drive back to the tiny town of Granite Gulch. She continued to remain strong after her brother left her at her apartment door.

She'd lived in the apartment about a month before she'd left to travel to the Colton Valley Ranch to retrieve the watch, and the small one-bedroom place still didn't feel like home.

Tanner's suite had felt like home, not because of the place itself, but rather because of the man and his daughters. It was a home that had needed a wife and mother to complete it.

She unpacked her clothing and fixed herself a microwave dinner from the freezer. She ate the tasteless meal while thinking about all the meals she'd shared with Tanner and the twins.

She threw the container in the trash and then went into the tiny bathroom and showered. As the hot water spray pummeled her skin, she remembered Tanner's soft, caressing touch as they'd made love.

Every thought, every memory, was wrapped in a welcoming fog that kept her from actually feeling.

She remained in the shower until the water turned tepid, and only then did she dry off and change into a nightshirt.

It was only when she was in bed that she allowed herself to really think…to really feel once again. Tears burned her eyes as deep sobs choked in the back of her throat. She let them loose. She allowed her grief over saying goodbye to her dreams to consume her.

She finally fell into an exhausted sleep that was haunted by visions of a blue-splattered fence and a mother who wouldn't wake up and a man who refused to love her.

Morning came late for her. She was shocked to open her eyes, glance at her alarm clock on the nightstand and realize it was after nine.

There were no sweet babies to wake her up this

morning, with their half sentences and funny gibberish. There was no joy in slicing bits of fruit and cutting buttery toast in half. Happy little laughter didn't fill the air and no deep male voice caressed her senses with a sweet greeting.

Eventually she knew the pain would lose its intensity, but Tanner had been wrong if he thought she could ever forget him. He was burned into her heart, into her very soul, with a fire that had forever marked her.

Someday maybe she would fall in love again. Her heart would eventually heal enough to allow that to happen, but there would always be a scar left behind by Tanner.

She got out of bed and shuffled into the bathroom, where the watch sat on the counter next to the sink. Today she would see her father for the very last time.

Any hopes and dreams she might have ever entertained about having a loving father would finally be put to rest…just like she had to put to rest any dreams she'd had about sharing her life with Tanner and Leigh and Lily.

One day at a time, one foot in front of the other—that was how she needed to cope with life right now. And right now the only thing she wanted done was to get the watch to her father.

A little over an hour later she pulled up in front of the Blackthorn County Prison. It was a grim place with guard towers and barbed wire and the aura of hopelessness she imagined clung to all prisons.

Her heart beat just a little faster as she anticipated the meeting with her father. Would he be calm and rational? Sometimes visits with him could be contentious and Matthew would be irrational.

She had no idea what to anticipate from him if he opened the back of the watch and discovered his little map was gone. Trevor had intended to put it back into the watch, but when they'd gotten back to the suite after the shoot-out at the silos, the map had been gone. It had apparently fallen out of Trevor's back pocket in all the chaos. Surely Matthew wouldn't be angry, especially given the fact that all the map had led to was a getaway cache of sorts. There had been no big treasure for anyone to find.

It didn't take long for her to get through all the security measures, but instead of being accompanied to where her father had been the last time she'd seen him, she was taken to an office where the warden awaited her.

"Ms. Colton," he said and rose from his desk with a solemn expression. "I just got off the phone with your brother Trevor. I called him to let him know that your father passed away sometime early this morning."

Josie stared at him and waited for some sort of grief to overtake her. But there was no real grief, only a sad acceptance that Matthew Colton had died alone in a prison because of the choices he'd made in his life.

She thanked the warden and left the prison. Her

father was gone, along with her mother. But they'd left behind children who were strong and good, people who Josie was proud to call her family.

It was finally time for her to build a new life, a life without fear, a life without Tanner.

It was a beautiful day. For the past four days there had been a slight respite in the intense heat, and the white tent in the cemetery provided shade that made the temperature even more comfortable.

The Granite Gulch Cemetery wasn't big and fancy, but it was the right place to lay Matthew Colton to rest. Trevor had made sure he'd been buried with the watch he'd insisted to the end held sentimental value to him.

The funeral had been short and nobody had attended except Matthew's children. They hadn't wanted anything but a private affair. There were no gawkers, nobody to pick up a piece of dirt or anything else and sell it as a piece of serial-killer memorabilia on the internet.

Now that the ceremony was over and the minister had gone, Josie and her siblings all stood around as if reluctant to leave each other's company.

"How are you holding up?" Josie's sister, Annabel, threw an arm around Josie's shoulder.

"As well as anyone," she replied. "And how are you doing?" She cast a meaningful glance to Jesse Willard, the farmer who had captured Annabel's heart.

In fact, all of Josie's siblings had significant others with them. They had found the partners they wanted to spend the rest of their lives with, and while Josie was happy for all of them, she couldn't help but think of Tanner and what might have been.

But it had been five long days since she'd said goodbye and driven away from the Colton Valley Ranch. There had been no phone call from him, nothing to indicate he had any regrets about how things had ended between them.

She could only hope for the best for him. She hoped he found a wonderful nanny for the twins. And she could only wish that someday he might find some woman to love who could be the partner for him that she couldn't be. She wanted love for him and the girls, even if it wouldn't be with her.

"Ethan is having everyone back to his ranch for a meal," Annabel said, pulling Josie from her thoughts. "Lizzie had the diner bring in a ton of food for the occasion. You're coming, right?"

Josie nodded and glanced over at Lizzie, who had recently given birth and positively glowed with happiness. Ethan gazed at Lizzie just like Josie had believed Tanner looked at her. Had it all just been in her imagination? Had she just wanted it so badly she'd seen it when it hadn't been there?

"Josie?" Annabel said.

"Yes, I'm coming. It's nice when all of us can get together," she replied.

Annabel smiled. "It's been a long time coming.

We'd all begun to wonder if we'd ever see you again."
Annabel pulled her into a hug. "It's nice to finally
have you home, where you belong."

Josie clung to her sister for a long moment, and as
their embrace broke up, she thought she saw somebody standing just behind a nearby tree.

Every muscle in her body tensed and her heart
began to thrum a rhythm of danger. What now? Was
there somebody else who wanted to hurt her? Maybe
one of Desmond's old buddies had flown under the
radar and had hunted her down after all these years.

She was about to call to one of her brothers when
the man stepped out from behind the tree. The sunlight glinted in his blond hair and Josie's heart leaped
to her throat.

Tanner.

What was he doing here?

"Are we ready to go?" Trevor asked everyone.

"You all go ahead. I'll catch up later," Josie said.

She remained standing in place as everyone began to
leave the tent area and head to their cars. She watched
until the last of their cars had disappeared from view
and then she turned back to where Tanner stood, obviously waiting to speak with her.

She didn't want her heart to beat so wildly in her
chest at the mere sight of him. She didn't want the rush
of love that cascaded through her as she approached
where he stood, so tall, so handsome and so very
solemn.

"Tanner," she said, grateful her voice betrayed none of the raging emotions inside her.

"I heard about your father's death. I wanted to tell you I'm sorry for your loss."

Was that why he had come here? To offer his support in case she was grieving? "Thank you, but we all knew it was coming," she replied.

He shifted his weight from one foot to the other. "How are things at the ranch?" she asked, simply to fill the awkward moment.

"Tense. As you probably know from the news reports, Eldridge is still missing and no ransom note has been received."

"I haven't been watching the news," she replied. She hadn't wanted to see anything that had to do with the ranch where she had found love, where she had found the place she belonged. She'd known that watching any of those news reports would only make her think of him. "It looks like your eye has healed up nicely."

He reached up and touched his eyebrow and then dropped his hand back to his side. "It's fine."

She wanted to scream. She wanted to throw herself into his arms. Their conversation was stilted and painful and she almost resented his presence here.

"How are Lily and Leigh?" Agony. She was in sheer agony as she thought of the little girls who had won her heart so quickly.

Tanner shoved his hands in his pockets. "Peggy

has been taking care of them, but they miss you. I miss you."

Josie stared at him. For the first time she saw the shadows of sleepless nights beneath his eyes, the strain that lined his forehead. She didn't speak. She was afraid to hope. Whatever happened next was entirely up to him.

"I miss you, Josie. I thought we'd be fine without you. I wanted to be fine, but you haunt me every hour of every day. You were right when you told me I was afraid. I've been afraid to move on with my life, scared of embracing or believing in your love."

He pulled his hands from his pockets and slicked one through his hair. "After doing a lot of soul-searching, I realized it wasn't so much that you were young that bothered me. It was the fear that I could never be enough for you that made me afraid."

Josie's heart raced, but still she remained in place and said nothing. She needed him to reach for her. He had to tell her that he wanted her in his life forever. She wouldn't settle for anything else.

"Wait here," he said and then walked over to the tree he'd been standing behind when she'd first seen him. He disappeared from her sight for a moment and when he reappeared his arms were filled with long-stemmed red roses.

"On the day Marceline brought you those friendship roses, you told me they were the first ones you'd ever received. I want to be the first man to give you red roses for love and I want to be the last man to give you red roses for love."

His eyes held a wealth of emotions—hot desire, combined with a depth of caring and love...sweet love. "I realize now that you were right—age doesn't matter. I also realize my broken marriage to Helen wasn't totally my fault. I am man enough to make a woman happy. I'm more than man enough to make you happy for the rest of your life. All that really matters is love and I love you. I want you to be my wife, Josie. I want you to be my partner and raise my daughters and give me more children and grow old with me."

"For goodness' sake, put those roses down and take me in your arms," Josie replied. Tears of happiness blurred her vision and her entire body trembled with the need to be in his embrace.

He tossed the flowers to the ground and pulled her against him. He took her mouth with his, kissing her with an intensity that stole her breath and rushed a welcome fiery heat through her body.

When the kiss ended he continued to hold her tight. For the first time in her entire life she felt safe and loved. He stroked a hand down her cheek and smiled.

"You're the bravest woman I've ever met. You make me want to be brave and strong for you and for my daughters," he said. "I believed that maybe you were staying with me at the ranch because you were afraid to face your life out of protective custody. Now I know that I've been hiding out at the ranch, afraid to get on with my own life. I've realized I'm ready to make a move. It's time for me to get on with my life the way I'd always dreamed."

She looked up at him and placed a hand on his cheek. "Whatever you do, I'll be beside you. Wherever you go, I want to be there."

"I've found a ranch." His eyes were filled with the shine of new possibilities. "It has a beautiful four-bedroom house and enough land to sustain a herd of cattle. I think you'll like it. It's right here in Granite Gulch."

She gasped in surprise. "Really? Are you sure that's what you want?"

"I want my wife to have her family close to her. What do you think, Josie-love? Will you marry me and we'll live on our ranch and raise our children together?"

"Yes, oh, yes, Tanner."

Once again his lips took hers and his arms tightened around her. Josie-love. He'd called her Josie-love and she couldn't wait to build their future together. Tanner-love. Josie-love. Lily-love and Leigh-love. His family and now hers.

The fact that he had looked for a place in Granite Gulch, knowing she wanted to bond with her siblings, was the icing on the cake.

Although most people would think it odd that she'd been proposed to in a cemetery following her serial-

killer father's funeral, Josie didn't care. It was odd…
Her entire life had been odd and crazy.

But one thing she knew with certainty—this man
was her future. With him, she was finally home.

Epilogue

Troy Watkins was ready to fire half his staff, punch a couple of reporters in the nose and drink himself into oblivion, but he wasn't going to do any of those things.

The idea that he even had such wild thoughts was a sign the Colton case was positively eating him alive. It was nearly midnight, way past time for him to be home and in his bed, but a good night's sleep had become a luxury denied to him since the day he'd been called out to Colton Valley Ranch to investigate the missing Eldridge.

Nobody had been able to get Marceline Colton to talk, and she and Fowler and Whitney all remained at the top of the suspect list, but so far no evidence had come to light to conclusively point a finger of guilt to any specific person.

And if those three weren't suspicious enough, there were other family members and staff and business associates who all had to be cleared one by one.

A dedicated tip line had been set up, but so far all it had yielded was a reminder to Troy that there were some crazy nuts out there. Still, each and every tip had to be chased down, no matter how crazy it sounded.

He now got up from his desk and reached for his hat. Time to go home, where he'd lie in bed with racing thoughts keeping sleep at bay.

And the one thought that would haunt him until he got an answer was, where was Eldridge? And if the man was dead, then where in the hell was his body?

* * * * *

REQUEST YOUR FREE BOOKS!
2 FREE NOVELS PLUS 2 FREE GIFTS!

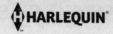

ROMANTIC suspense

Sparked by danger, fueled by passion

YES! Please send me 2 FREE Harlequin® Romantic Suspense novels and my 2 FREE gifts (gifts are worth about $10). After receiving them, if I don't wish to receive any more books, I can return the shipping statement marked "cancel." If I don't cancel, I will receive 4 brand-new novels every month and be billed just $4.74 per book in the U.S. or $5.49 per book in Canada. That's a savings of at least 12% off the cover price! It's quite a bargain! Shipping and handling is just 50¢ per book in the U.S. and 75¢ per book in Canada.* I understand that accepting the 2 free books and gifts places me under no obligation to buy anything. I can always return a shipment and cancel at any time. Even if I never buy another book, the two free books and gifts are mine to keep forever.

240/340 HDN GH3P

Name	(PLEASE PRINT)	

Address		Apt. #

City	State/Prov.	Zip/Postal Code

Signature (if under 18, a parent or guardian must sign)

Mail to the **Reader Service:**

IN U.S.A.: P.O. Box 1867, Buffalo, NY 14240-1867
IN CANADA: P.O. Box 609, Fort Erie, Ontario L2A 5X3

**Want to try two free books from another line?
Call 1-800-873-8635 or visit www.ReaderService.com.**

* Terms and prices subject to change without notice. Prices do not include applicable taxes. Sales tax applicable in N.Y. Canadian residents will be charged applicable taxes. Offer not valid in Quebec. This offer is limited to one order per household. Not valid for current subscribers to Harlequin Romantic Suspense books. All orders subject to credit approval. Credit or debit balances in a customer's account(s) may be offset by any other outstanding balance owed by or to the customer. Please allow 4 to 6 weeks for delivery. Offer available while quantities last.

Your Privacy—The Reader Service is committed to protecting your privacy. Our Privacy Policy is available online at www.ReaderService.com or upon request from the Reader Service.

We make a portion of our mailing list available to reputable third parties that offer products we believe may interest you. If you prefer that we not exchange your name with third parties, or if you wish to clarify or modify your communication preferences, please visit us at www.ReaderService.com/consumerschoice or write to us at Reader Service Preference Service, P.O. Box 9062, Buffalo, NY 14240-9062. Include your complete name and address.

HRS15

Her voice sounded oddly hollow. "Something wrong?" he asked, doubling back.

Mirabella turned the monitor so he could see the screen more readily. The anonymous email sender was back. He glanced at the time stamp and saw the email had been sent out early this morning. It was the first thing she had seen when she'd opened her computer.

"What new bridegroom is getting away with murder?" the first line read. "Better be careful and watch your back, Mirabella, or you might be next on his list."

Anger spiked within him. Zane bit back a number of choice words. Cursing at the sender, or at her computer, would accomplish exactly nothing. He needed to take some kind of effective action, not merely rail impotently at shadows.

Zane put his hand on her shoulder in a protective gesture.

"Don't be afraid, Belle. I'm going to track this infantile scum down. I won't let him get to you."

He meant physically, but she took it to mean mentally. "He's already gotten to me, but I'm not afraid," she fired back. "I'm angry. This jerk has no right to try to say what he's saying, to try to poison people's minds against us." Her eyes flashed as she turned toward Zane. "What the hell is his game?"

Her normally porcelain cheeks were flushed with suppressed fury. He'd never seen her look so angry—nor so desirable. Instead of becoming incensed, which he knew was what this anonymous vermin was after, Zane felt himself becoming aroused. By Mirabella.

Now wasn't the time, he upbraided himself.

It was *never* going to be the time, he reminded himself in the next moment. He'd married her to save her reputation, to squelch the hurtful, damaging rumors. Stringing up the person saying all those caustic things about them, about *her*, did not lead to the "and they all lived happily ever after" ending he was after—even if it might prove to be immensely satisfying on a very primal level.

Nothing wrong with a little primal once in a while, Zane caught himself thinking as his thoughts returned to last night.